OUT AT HOME

Also by Cal Ripken, Jr.
with Kevin Cowherd

Hothead
Super Slugger
Wild Pitch
Squeeze Play
The Closer

a novel by

CAL RIPKEN, JR.

with Kevin Cowherd

𝒟ɪsɴᴇʏ • HYPERION

Los Angeles   New York

A special thanks, as always, to Stephanie Owens Lurie, associate publisher
of Disney • Hyperion, for her invaluable guidance and sublime editing skills.
She makes us look better than we are. Way better.
—K.C.

First Hardcover Edition, March 2015
First Paperback Edition, March 2016
10 9 8 7 6 5 4 3 2 1
FAC-025438-15349
Printed in the United States of America

SUSTAINABLE
FORESTRY
INITIATIVE

Certified Chain of Custody
Promoting Sustainable Forestry

www.sfiprogram.org
SFI-01054

The SFI label applies to the text stock

ISBN 978-1-4847-2789-8
Library of Congress Control Number for Hardcover: 2014027377

Visit www.DisneyBooks.com

To Nancy, still the greatest of all time.
—*Kevin Cowherd*

Mickey Labriogla took the screaming foul tip smack in the middle of his catcher's mask, the ball ricocheting with such force that it bounced halfway to the pitcher's mound. The blow rocked him flat on his back as the rest of the Orioles gasped.

Showtime, Mickey thought. *Here we go. Make it an instant classic.*

Clutching his head with both hands, he climbed slowly to his feet and staggered in circles like a drunk. Finally he collapsed facedown in a dusty heap at the feet of the batter, Katelyn Morris, who regarded him suspiciously.

"Is he . . . *dead*?" third baseman Hunter Carlson asked as the Orioles ran over to check on their catcher.

Katelyn poked at Mickey's shoulder with one of her cleats and snorted.

"I doubt it," she said. "He's probably not even hurt. It hit him in the head, didn't it? We *know* there's nothing to hurt in there."

Suddenly Mickey scrambled to his feet. Raising his

hands over his head and bouncing on his toes like a victorious boxer, he flashed a wide grin.

"Ladies and gentlemen, I don't believe what I'm seeing!" he intoned in a dramatic announcer's voice. "Michael J. Labriogla just took a vicious foul ball to the face, a shot that would have laid out a water buffalo, never mind any other young ballplayer in the country. But here he is, back on his feet and dancing! Oh, you talk about heart! You talk about courage! No, they don't come any tougher than this young man!"

"They don't come any dumber, either," Katelyn muttered, shaking her head. "Okay, you've had your little fun—as pathetic and sophomoric as it was. Can we get on with batting practice now?"

Mickey pulled up his mask and gazed at Katelyn with a hurt expression.

"I hope you don't talk like that when we're dating," he said. "What would the other kids think?"

"Yeah, like that could ever happen," Katelyn said, rolling her eyes. "Keep dreaming, nerd."

She dug in at the plate again and called out to the pitcher's mound, where Coach Labriogla, Mickey's dad, looked on with amusement. "Coach, could you puh-leeze throw another pitch so I don't have to listen to any more of this ridiculous blabbering?"

The rest of the Orioles cracked up as Mickey snickered and crouched down for the next pitch.

He was a big, blocky twelve-year-old—he'd shot up two inches and gained fifteen pounds since last season, much of it around his belly, which had left him feeling more than a little self-conscious. But he was a handsome kid, with a thatch of red hair and freckles, and a smile that seemed permanently in place. And on this perfect July morning, with the sun shining brightly and the sky so blue it seemed painted, he was in his usual terrific mood.

There was no place on earth Mickey wanted to be more than where he was right now, behind home plate on a dusty baseball diamond with his teammates.

A lot of kids hated catching. They hated wearing the bulky protective gear on hot summer days. They hated the constant squatting and all the punishment a catcher took from foul tips, wild pitches in the dirt, and the occasional bone-rattling collision at the plate.

Not Mickey. He loved everything about the position. He loved being involved in every pitch and seeing the entire game unfold before him. He loved calling pitches and trying to outthink the hitter in the age-old mental chess game that was every at-bat since the beginning of time.

His dad had told him that back in the day, ballplayers used to refer to the catcher's mask, chest protector, and shin guards as "the tools of ignorance."

But Mickey wore the catcher's gear proudly. He put on each piece with all the solemn ritual of a knight donning a suit of armor for battle. Before each game he would lovingly lay out his equipment on the dugout bench. Sometimes he would even narrate as each item was affixed to his body:

"Step one, as the great catcher prepares to lay his chiseled physique on the line once again for his team, he first secures his shin guards, using a crossover pattern with the straps, and making sure each fits snugly . . ."

"Really?" Katelyn once snapped at him. "We have to listen to play-by-play of you putting on your stupid gear?"

"Step two," Mickey had continued, ignoring the O's right fielder, "he carefully positions the chest protector. After the protective cup, which he dons in private for obvious reasons"—here he shot a knowing glance at Katelyn, the only girl on the team—"and the face mask designed to ensure that his rugged, movie-star good looks aren't damaged, the chest protector is key."

"That's it, I'm going to hurl," Katelyn said, stomping away to much laughter before she had to listen to Mickey expound on the virtues of his oversize catcher's mitt and how much he loved it.

Today, even though Mickey was in his usual sunny mood, a palpable air of worry hung over the Orioles as practice continued.

Not only were they only slightly better than a .500 team now, but their best pitcher and Mickey's lifelong friend, Gabe Vasquez, had hurt his shoulder in last week's 4–2 win over the Tigers. Rumors were already circulating that Gabe was done for the season. No one had heard anything official from Gabe or his parents, though, which left the Orioles hoping their ace would be back at some point.

Without Gabe, the Orioles would definitely struggle. True, they played solid defense. And the heart of their batting order—shortstop Sammy Noah, Katelyn, center fielder Corey Maduro, and Mickey himself—had as much power as any other lineup in the league.

In fact, the Orioles had so much swagger about their ability to give the ball a ride that they'd sometimes flex their biceps and chant, "MOVE THE FENCES BACK! IT'S TOO EASY!" during games, earning death stares from Coach.

No wonder the rest of the league doesn't like us, Mickey thought.

The Orioles didn't mean to be cocky—they were just staying loose and having fun. But Mickey knew it rubbed some of the other teams the wrong way. And it definitely ticked off their coaches—you could tell by the way they shook their heads and muttered.

But the Orioles would need to hit a ton of homers, Mickey knew, if Gabe was lost for the season. He was one of the best pitchers in the league, and also a team leader with a quiet self-confidence that rubbed off on the other Orioles. The O's number two pitcher, Danny Connolly, while steady, lacked the intimidating fastball and all-around mound presence of Gabe.

No, without Gabe, the Orioles had no shot at the championship, Mickey believed. No shot at all.

There was an added incentive for the O's to win it all this year: the league champs would play in a new one-game, winner-take-all regional final against the powerful Huntington Yankees. The Yankees were the most famous—*infamous* was probably a better word—twelve-and-under team in the area, perennial winners of their league title.

Every Oriole had heard tales of the Huntington Yankees. They were reputed to be a bunch of spoiled rich kids, a team of All-Stars handpicked by their coach, Al "Money" Mayhew.

The gruff Mayhew was renowned not only for bending the rules in assembling his dream team each season, but also for using questionable tactics during games. Like having two of his favorites yell put-downs at opposing batters to distract them, and having his batters constantly step out of the batter's box to disrupt the opposing pitcher's timing.

"Definitely need you back if we play Huntington, Big Gabe," Mickey whispered as he eased out of his gear before it was his turn to hit.

Danny was throwing BP now, Mickey's dad having begged off with a sore arm a few minutes earlier. Mickey watched the last of Danny's pitches to Corey. Each one seemed to cross the plate belt-high at exactly the same speed. His dad called them "assembly-line fastballs," each an exact replica of the one before it.

Each practically screaming, "Hit me!"

Danny was one of the most popular players on the Orioles. But seeing the way Corey was swinging from his heels and sending rockets to the deepest parts of the outfield, Mickey was even more convinced it would be a brutal last quarter of the season if the Orioles had to go without Gabe.

As Mickey got loose in the on-deck circle with a few practice swings, something on the adjacent field caught his eye. He looked over to see his dad crouched behind home plate, catching for a tall kid with long brown hair and a cap pulled low over his eyes.

The boy had a smooth relaxed windup with a high leg kick, yet the ball seemed to explode out of his hand. Mickey watched transfixed as the kid threw half a dozen fastballs, each one darting and dancing and smacking into his dad's mitt with a loud *WHUMP!*

With each pitch, the kid's grim expression never changed. All business, Mickey thought. Must be a lot of fun at parties.

"Curve!" the kid barked, and the next pitch spun and broke sharply at the last second, Mickey's dad scooping it out of the dirt and chortling with glee.

Mickey whistled softly. That's some filthy stuff, he thought. I don't know who that kid plays for. But whoever it is, the catcher's glove hand must sting for days.

By now some of the other Orioles were watching this little drama, too. Corey had stepped out of the batter's box, his eyes widening with each pitch the kid threw. Danny and Katelyn were also studying the boy, obviously impressed.

A moment later, Mickey's dad stood, signaling an end to the session, and the kid nodded. As the two of them walked toward the rest of the Orioles, Mickey's dad grinned widely. The tall boy remained stone-faced.

"Boys and girls," his dad said to the team, "meet Zach Winslow. Looks like we've got ourselves a new pitcher."

The tall boy spit a shower of sunflower seeds into the air and pounded the pocket of his glove with his fist. He looked intently from one puzzled face to another and smirked.

"Guys, this is your lucky day," he said. "You just won yourselves the championship."

Coach got to the bad news quickly, as he usually did.

"I'm afraid Gabe's season is over," he said. "His mom left a message on my cell earlier. He has a severe elbow strain. And his doctor said that if he doesn't rest it, he could do permanent damage."

The Orioles groaned and looked disconsolately at one another.

"That's it, we're doomed!" said Hunter, throwing up his hands. "All life is over. We'll never win again. Oh, this is bad—real *bad*! We're gonna go, like, oh-for-the-rest-of-the-season."

"Thanks for that vote of confidence," Danny said drily. "Much appreciated. Great for the ego. I'm feeling much better about myself."

Katelyn glared at Hunter. Then she hauled off and punched him in the shoulder.

"Man up, nerd!" she barked. "We are *not* doomed. Any more whining out of you, and I'll smack you somewhere on that puny little body that'll hurt a whole lot more."

The rest of the Orioles snickered. Hunter rubbed his shoulder and stared sullenly at Katelyn but said nothing.

"Are we done with all the drama?" Mickey's dad said. "Can I continue? Okay, now for the good news. The league knows we desperately need another pitcher—no offense, Danny, we still need you, and you'll still get a lot of work. But since Zach and his family just moved here, they're letting us have him as an emergency fill-in."

Coach's grin got even wider. He rubbed his hands together gleefully.

"'Course, I don't think the league knows how good he is," he went on. "Some of you may have seen him throwing to me just now. I can say without fear of exaggeration that the boy's got a live arm. A *real* live arm. Yep, I think we're going to enjoy having Zach on this team. Right, Zach?"

"Call me Zoom," the tall boy said.

The Orioles looked at each other.

"Zoom?" Katelyn said. "That's not a name. That's, like, a sound."

"Yeah," Sammy said. "Wasn't there a commercial about a car that went zoom-zoom?"

Zoom shrugged. "I don't watch much TV," he said. "Too busy working on my game. I'm all about perfecting my craft, being the best pitcher I can be."

As the rest of the Orioles made gagging sounds, Katelyn said, "Puh-leeze! Tell me you're kidding with that answer."

"Nope," the kid went on. "Anyway, *zoom* is the sound my fastball makes. And it's on you so fast, you only hear one *zoom* before it handcuffs you."

"Oh . . . my . . . God!" Katelyn said, looking at the others. "He's *serious*!"

Zoom stared at her. His expression remained blank as he spewed another stream of sunflower seeds into the air.

For several seconds, no one spoke.

"Well," Mickey's dad said finally, "I'll leave you all to get acquainted. I have to call Gabe's mom back, tell her how sorry we are and how much we'll miss Gabe. But I'll let her know we're going to be okay for the time being."

As soon as Coach was gone, the Orioles circled around the tall boy.

"So you're like, what, the best kid pitcher *ever*?" Katelyn said. "Is that what you're saying?"

"And you're guaranteeing we're going to win the league?" Sammy said. "You—Zach, Zoom, whatever your name is—you're personally going to save our season? Is that it?"

Hunter bowed in front of Zoom and murmured, "We are not worthy, Lord Zoom, we are not worthy . . ."

Zoom held up his hands and the hint of a smile appeared for the first time.

"Okay, okay, have your fun," he said. "But there's something you should know. And this should make you feel pretty good about our chances the rest of the way. Ready? Okay. I just got back from the Elite Arms Camp."

The Orioles looked at one another.

"The Elite *Farms* Camp?" Sammy said, nudging Corey. "How does learning how to milk a cow or feed chickens help you play baseball?"

As the rest of the Orioles cracked up, Zoom shook his

head sadly, as if dealing with a particularly dim-witted group of individuals.

"Elite *Arms*," he said. "It's the premier instructional camp for youth pitchers on the East Coast. You gotta be an off-the-charts prospect to attend. It's strictly by-invitation-only. *Everybody's* heard of Elite Arms."

"Everybody," Corey said, nodding to the others.

"Absolutely everybody," Sammy said.

"In China they've heard of it," Corey said. "India, Africa, Australia. All over the world."

"You know," said Spencer Dalton, the left fielder, "I think I heard the president talking about the camp during a news conference the other day. In fact, Zoom, I think he did a shout-out to you! No, now that I think about it, I'm *positive* he did. 'Major props to the kid who went to Elite Arms'—that's exactly what he said!"

Zoom's face turned red as the Orioles dissolved in laughter again. They were on a roll, teasing the new guy unmercifully, to the point where Mickey was starting to feel sorry for him.

Sure, the kid is coming across as a world-class dork, Mickey thought. But maybe he's really shy and trying a little too hard to impress his new teammates. Or maybe he's just talking trash because that's what kids on his previous team did and he thinks it's expected here, too.

At the same time, Mickey felt horrible for Gabe. Season over? He couldn't imagine it. Gabe was like him—he lived and breathed baseball all year long. What he *could* imagine—all too clearly—was Gabe sitting in the doctor's office, trying to hold back the tears as he heard the news.

Mickey shuddered. What a blow to the poor guy.

Plus the Orioles were losing more than just an awesome pitcher. Gabe was a great teammate, too, the kind of kid who was always encouraging everyone no matter what the score was or how well he himself was doing.

In fact, in the three years they'd played together, not once had Mickey ever heard Gabe talk about his own stats. All he seemed to care about was the Orioles winning.

Oh, yeah, Mickey thought, this new kid—Zoom, Zach, whatever—has big spikes to fill.

As practice went on, though, it was obvious that not only did Zoom Winslow look All-World on the mound, he was a pretty complete player. He showed good range running down fly balls in the outfield. And when it was his turn to hit, he sprayed line drives to all fields and showed decent power.

"The boy can play a little," Sammy admitted grudgingly, watching Zoom leg out a double on his last at-bat.

"Yeah," Hunter said, "but it's only practice. Let's see what happens in a real live game. Hope I don't have to start bowing to him again, though. That would majorly suck."

At the end of practice, Coach spoke briefly to the Orioles about their upcoming game against the Blue Jays and what time to be at the field. Mickey noticed that Zoom kept his head down the whole time, drawing big Zs in the dirt with the handle of his bat and barely paying attention.

When Coach dismissed them, Zoom tossed his bat in his gear bag and headed wordlessly for the parking lot. After a moment, Mickey followed him.

"Hey," he called out, "I'm Mickey, the catcher for this

homely-looking crew. Don't mind them—they're just getting to know you. You looked pretty good out there. Should be fun working with you."

Zoom stopped and studied Mickey.

"*Working* with me?" he said.

"Yeah, you know," Mickey said. "Going over the signs, figuring out what pitches to throw, how you like to pitch to different batters . . ."

Just then a black SUV pulled up. A kind-looking man with glasses and thinning hair was behind the wheel. He rolled down the window and waved at the two boys.

"Hold *on* a minute, Dad!" Zoom barked. "Jeez!"

He turned back to Mickey and his eyes narrowed.

"Look, big man," he said, "here's how we're going to *work* together: I pitch; you catch and stay out of the way. End of story."

With that, he opened the door and climbed into the front passenger seat. The driver smiled at Mickey and waved again as the car rolled away.

Ohhh-kay, Mickey thought as he watched the car disappear. This should be interesting. Very, very interesting.

Gabe rolled up the sleeve of his Orioles T-shirt and demanded that Mickey examine his arm.

"There!" Gabe said. "See anything wrong with it? Anything at all? No, right? No swelling, no black-and-blue, no nothing! It feels fine! But that stupid doctor says I can't pitch anymore!"

Mickey nodded, trying to appear sympathetic. But soon he returned his gaze to the walls of Gabe's bedroom and winced.

Gabe and his mom lived in a big old house on the outskirts of town, and Mrs. Vasquez had basically ceded decorating rights to her son's room the day they moved in. This turned out to be a bad move.

A *really* bad move.

The result was a crazy, jumbled montage of posters of big-league pitchers like Johnny Cueto, Félix Hernández, and Chris Tillman alongside young kick-butt rock guitarists like Jack White, Alexi Laiho, and Synyster Gates.

Every spare inch of wall and ceiling was covered with

posters. Even the windows were plastered with them, lending the room a dark, gloomy air.

Gabe called it his "Gabe-Cave" and said it was his own personal haven of tranquillity and inspiration. But Mickey wondered how anyone could live in the place without having a perpetual migraine from all the wild colors assaulting the eyes.

"I could go out there and pitch today," Gabe continued, his voice rising, "but the stupid doctor's got my mom brainwashed. The whole thing is ridiculous!"

He grabbed his glove off the desk and walked over to the full-length mirror on the wall. After studying his reflection for a moment, he went into his windup, pretended to uncork a fastball—and promptly yelped in pain, grabbing his elbow.

"Yeah, you're fine, all right," Mickey said. "What's the matter with that doctor? Where'd he get his medical degree from, anyway? Saying you have something wrong with your arm? What a quack that guy is!"

"Shut up," Gabe growled. "Whose side are you on, anyway?"

He slammed his glove on the floor and plopped morosely on his bed. He put his hands behind his head and stared up at the ceiling.

"A couple days of ice and rest and I'd be fine," he muttered. "Instead, I have to miss the whole second half of the season. And the dumb doctor didn't even X-ray the elbow! Shouldn't you at least take X-rays before making a diagnosis that ruins a kid's life forever?"

"Well, at least you're not overreacting," Mickey said, grinning. He ducked quickly as Gabe fired a pillow at his head.

It was the day after the Orioles practice and Mickey had stopped by to see if he could cheer up Gabe. His plan wasn't working out too well so far.

Briefly, Mickey recounted the events of the previous day's workout, including the surprise announcement that a new kid named Zach Winslow with a real live arm was now the O's number one pitcher.

Looking at Gabe's downcast expression, Mickey wasn't sure what bothered his bud more: the fact that he was done for the year, or the fact that he had been replaced so easily with a hotshot who could blow batters away with an eighty-mile-per-hour heater.

"Oh," Mickey said, "I should probably tell you this, too. The new guy calls himself Zoom."

Gabe rolled on his side and cocked an eyebrow. *"Zoo?"*

"No, *Zoom*," Mickey corrected. "Z-o-o-m."

"And that would be because . . . ?" Gabe said. "Go ahead. Explain the crazy name."

Mickey shrugged and returned his gaze to the jumble of posters. He was alarmed to see that they were even sprouting in Gabe's closet now.

"He said something about his fastball, the sound it makes when it blows past the batter," Mickey replied with a shrug. "He also made a big point of telling us that he'd just come back from this fancy pitching camp. Elite Arms, I think it was."

"Oh, great, GREAT!" Gabe said, jumping to his feet and

throwing his hands in the air. "A pitching phenom who's also had the finest instruction a kid could ask for! Well, I can see the team won't be needing *me* anymore."

He paced around the room, growing more and more agitated.

"Yeah," he continued, "by next week, you guys'll be like: 'Remember that big wuss who used to pitch for us? The loser who hurt his elbow? Gabe Something, wasn't it? Whatever happened to that big dork?' "

Mickey rolled his eyes.

"Seriously?" he said. "You really need to chill, dude."

But Gabe was in no mood for chilling. Instead, he moved quickly to his desk, opened his laptop, and typed in a few words.

"What are you doing?" Mickey asked. "I *know* you're not checking on your summer reading list. You do that about an hour before the first day of school, right?"

"You, my friend, are hysterical," Gabe said, without looking up.

He tapped a few more keys and let out a low moan.

"Found it. Here's the camp's Web site," he said, reading from the screen. " 'Elite Arms: When you're ready to take your game to the next level—and beyond!' Oh, great, it's only the top freaking pitching camp on the East Coast! Look at this ad: 'We guarantee to add ten miles per hour to your fastball in one week!'

"That's it—I can't take any more," he said, lurching back to his bed and burying his face in his pillow.

Mickey took Gabe's place in front of the computer.

"I wonder if . . ." he began. It didn't take him long, just

a few clicks of the mouse, to find what he was looking for.

There it was: a big photo of Zoom, rearing back and firing to a batter who couldn't have appeared more terrified if they were throwing him into a shark tank.

In another photo, Zoom was calmly fielding what looked to be a bouncer back to the mound. And yet another shot showed him punching the air in triumph, presumably after racking up yet another strikeout.

"That's *him*, isn't it?" Gabe whispered.

He had materialized over Mickey's shoulder and was staring at the screen with a mixture of dread and fascination.

"Don't tell me he was named the camp's MVP, too," Gabe went on. "*Please* don't tell me that. I'm begging you. I can't take that kind of psychological pain."

"No," Mickey said, continuing to search the site, "there's no mention of him winning an award . . . oops, sorry. Spoke too soon."

He clicked on a fourth photo; this one showed Zoom holding a gleaming silver trophy on which was engraved MOST PROMISING CAMPER.

At this, Gabe let out a strangled cry and flopped on his bed again.

"Let me guess: he's a straight-A student, bound for Harvard, and he dates Kate Upton, too, right?" he wailed.

"Doesn't say anything about Kate Upton," Mickey said. "Think he just got tired of supermodels. You know how that gets old. Oh, wait, no wonder! It says he's dating Jennifer Lawrence now."

"You're killing me," Gabe said, his eyes closed. "Just freakin' killing me."

A few minutes later, he sat up again. He rubbed his face and shook his head vigorously, as if shaking off a bad dream.

"Okay, major attitude change needed here," he said. "Sorry for the whine-fest. My season's over, and I just have to deal with it. But if this new guy can help us win, then he's a great get for the team. And I'm glad we have him. No, really."

Mickey chuckled to himself. The old Gabe was back, the selfless teammate who cared about winning more than anything else. His rant of self-pity had been totally uncharacteristic, and apparently it was behind him now.

This was another reason Mickey admired his bud so much. If a doctor told me my season was over, he thought, I'd be moping and sulking for weeks—if I didn't throw myself in front of a train first.

As Gabe puttered around the room, putting his glove and Orioles uniform away, Mickey continued to study the Elite Arms site.

There was no question that Zoom had been a superstar during his stay at the camp—how else to explain his four prominent photos on the site? A kid with a rag arm didn't get marquee treatment like that at a prestigious pitching camp.

Still, there was something about the photos that seemed strange to Mickey . . .

For a moment or two, he couldn't put his finger on it.

Then it came to him: not once, in any of the four shots, was Zoom smiling.

Even in the photo of him holding his trophy, he wore a serious expression. There were two other people in the shot—an older man wearing a red Elite Arms polo shirt and khaki pants, who looked to be a camp official, and a kid on crutches. And both of them were beaming.

How weird was it, Mickey thought, that both the geezer and the kid with the broken leg or whatever looked like they were having a better time than Zoom?

Wasn't baseball supposed to be *fun*?

If you went to a top-flight pitching camp and threw lights-out to the point where everybody was talking about how great you were and how much potential you had, and then they handed you a big silver cup with your name on it, and everyone was clapping and cheering and treating you like you were a major celebrity or something, wouldn't that be the greatest feeling in the whole world?

Wouldn't you be smiling like it was Christmas morning? Maybe Christmas morning times one hundred?

And wouldn't that smile be plastered to your big fat face for days and days afterward? Sure it would.

So what was up with this kid?

Mickey didn't know. But he had a feeling he'd find out soon enough.

Sammy stared at the garage door, its white paint pockmarked with dozens of dents and dark smudges, and turned back to Mickey.

"Say that again? You want me to *what*?" he asked.

"Throw some balls at my feet," Mickey said. "Hard as you can, too. Don't hold back."

Sammy studied Mickey's face to see if he was joking. When it was clear that he wasn't, Sammy shook his head softly.

"You're one sick kid, you know that?" he said. "Who does this on a ninety-degree day? Maybe you heard: they have this thing called air-conditioning. It's really not a brand-new invention, either. Been around a few years.

"Think about it, bro," he continued, draping an arm around Mickey. "We could be inside your nice cool house right now, slamming lemonade and playing video games. Wouldn't that be more fun than"—he swept his hand back to the garage door and frowned—*"this?"*

"I bet Moose Mayhew, that big dude who catches for the Huntington Yankees, does this drill," Mickey said.

Sammy snickered.

"If he does," he said, "it's probably in a special air-conditioned workout wing of his mansion. Or, if he's outside, he probably has a butler fanning him the whole time."

Mickey grinned. Sammy wasn't the first kid to question his sanity. But with the next Orioles game still a couple of days away, Mickey was determined to practice blocking pitches in the dirt—or in this case, blocking pitches in the asphalt. With the big garage door as his personal backstop.

It was one of his favorite drills, and he tried to do it two or three times a week. Despite his size, he was surprisingly nimble behind the plate and prided himself on being able to stop any pitch, no matter how wild.

But lately it had been hard to find someone to throw to him. His dad was always willing, but most days he came home too late from his job at the insurance agency to help out.

Gabe had helped Mickey with the drill many times, too. Except he was out of the picture now with that bad elbow—unless Mickey wanted the whole neighborhood to hear Gabe yelp in pain with each throw. Katelyn lived close by, but she was so sick of doing the drill, he couldn't ask her again.

Therefore, Mickey's new plan was to call random team-mates and invite them to hang out at his house for a couple of hours. When they showed up, he'd answer the door in full catcher's gear, which was strange enough.

Then he'd lead them out to his backyard, hand them a bucket of balls, and say, "Throw those at me like you're the wildest pitcher in history."

His little scheme didn't always go over well.

Like today.

"Let's talk this whole thing over," Sammy said. "Don't your mom and dad care about what you're doing to the garage door? Look at that thing. It's like it's been through a war. Like it's stopped cannonballs."

Mickey shook his head. "Nope, Mom and Dad are fine with it. It's a little deal I made with them. When the season's over, I bang the dents out and paint the door so it looks like new. And, if they ever change their minds about me using the door for drills, I can always come back with those two magic words. You know, the ones every parent wants to hear."

Sammy looked puzzled. "*What* two magic words?"

"*College scholarship,*" Mickey said with a grin. "I look at my parents with these big brown eyes and say, 'Hey, I'm working my butt off to save you guys tuition money down the road.' How can they turn me down after a line like that?"

He lowered his catcher's mask into place and pounded a fist in his mitt. "Okay, let's go. Enough with all the chatter. You think you're hot? It's like five hundred degrees with this gear on."

Sammy shrugged and lugged the bucket of balls over to the pitching rubber set up at the other end of the driveway. He picked up a ball and lobbed it at Mickey. The ball skipped about a foot in front of him and he gloved it easily.

He whipped off his mask and shot a disgusted look at Sammy.

"Dude," he said, "a second grader could have blocked

that one. That isn't doing me any good, okay? I need you to throw way harder than that. *Way* harder. I need to practice blocking balls with game-speed pitches. Understand? Now fire one in here."

Sammy rolled his eyes, but he did what he was told. He threw the next pitch as hard as he could at Mickey's feet.

The ball caromed off the asphalt and the big catcher lunged quickly to his right. He took the blow off his chest protector near his shoulder, grunting with satisfaction as he kept the ball in front of him.

In a real game, he thought, that little move right there might have saved a run—or at least prevented a runner on base from advancing on a wild pitch.

"Now you got it!" he shouted to Sammy. "Keep 'em coming like that!"

Sammy shook his head, but he reached for another ball and fired it even harder. This one bounced a foot in front of Mickey and caught him in the mask. When it dropped in front of him, he snatched it up and pretended to throw to second base as Sammy ducked.

"Okay, I'm two-for-two on blocks," Mickey said. "Let's do twenty-five of these and we'll call it a day."

Sammy gazed up at the broiling sun and wiped a hand across his forehead.

"Sure," he said. "Why go to a nice pool or water park when you can have this much fun? After all, neither of us has passed out from the heat yet."

Mickey grinned again and got back in his crouch. He couldn't blame Sammy for thinking he was losing his mind.

This was all about Mickey wanting to be the best catcher

in the league—it had been his goal for two years now. The only way he knew to accomplish that was to keep practicing, keep working on the fundamentals. He wanted to play in high school and he was serious about maybe someday winning a scholarship to play ball in college.

As his dad was always telling him, baseball teams at every level were always looking for good catchers. Mickey was also a solid hitter. But as his dad always said, if you were an outstanding defensive catcher with a good arm, teams would kill to have you on their roster—even if you couldn't hit a beach ball.

To be a standout catcher, Mickey knew, you needed the footwork of a matador behind the plate and the glove work of an NHL goalie. Mickey thought of himself as a bit of a baseball psychologist, too. He liked to study how the hitter set up in the batter's box and to try to guess what pitches he was comfortable handling and which ones would give him fits.

He studied the Orioles pitchers as much as he studied opposing batters. He could sense when a pitcher was overly excited and working too fast and needed to slow down. And he could read a pitcher's body language and tell when he needed encouragement, like when his head started to droop and he looked rattled in the midst of a rough inning.

"You need to be a Dr. Phil in shin guards to be a good catcher," his dad had told him, and Mickey had taken the advice to heart.

For the better part of twenty minutes, Sammy fired one errant fastball after another at Mickey until they were both soaked in perspiration and Mickey's face was the color of a ripe tomato. After the twenty-fifth pitch, he stood and waved his hands.

"Okay, that's enough for today," he said, breathing heavily.

Sammy mouthed a silent prayer of thanks and plopped down heavily on the grass in the shade of a pear tree.

"I thought it would never end," he said. "Please: lemonade. Water. Anything that's wet."

"Sure," Mickey said, peeling off his soggy chest protector. "But first we need to get our running in. The high school's just down the street. There's a big rubberized track right behind it. We'll do five or six miles, maybe some sprints, too. Then we'll get something to drink after that, promise."

Sammy stared at him in horror.

Mickey kept a straight face as long as he could.

"Kidding!" he said finally. "Let's go inside. How about some iced tea?"

Sammy grabbed Mickey's mitt and threw it at him. Then he jumped up and tackled him. The two of them fell down, laughing.

"You know something?" Sammy said. "You really *are* a sick kid!"

Mickey nodded.

"It's part of my charm," he said. "But look at it this way: we've got a big game against the Blue Jays Friday. And you just helped us get ready."

"And we didn't have to call an ambulance for either of us," Sammy said. "It doesn't get better than that, right?"

Mickey and his dad were the first to arrive at Eddie Murray Field for the Blue Jays game.

The sight of the old ballpark, with its freshly limed foul lines, immaculately trimmed grass, and infield dirt lovingly raked to a pebble-free reddish brown, never failed to make Mickey's heart race. He was so up for this game that he had changed into his uniform hours earlier. After that he'd spent forty-five minutes throwing a ball against the bounce-back machine in his backyard, just to work off the excess energy.

The rest of the Orioles seemed equally excited as they drifted in one by one and began loosening up. Gabe was there, too, in his full uni, going up to each player and slapping hands and getting them even more fired up.

There was just one problem.

The new hotshot pitcher they were counting on for the rest of the season was nowhere to be found.

At five thirty, when the Orioles took infield practice, there was still no sign of Zoom.

At five forty, twenty minutes before game time, Zoom had yet to arrive.

At five forty-two, the umpires were there. But Zoom wasn't.

Finally at five forty-five, a black SUV pulled up next to the field. The front passenger-side door opened and Zoom climbed out unhurriedly. The rear doors also opened and three boys who appeared to be Zoom's age jumped out.

One handed him his gear bag. The other gave him a water bottle. The third offered a towel. He nodded solemnly to each kid and they fell in behind him as he sauntered to the field.

The Orioles watched all this with rapt attention.

"Please tell me I'm seeing things," Katelyn said in a hushed tone. "Please tell me the kid doesn't *really* have an entourage."

"Unbelievable," Sammy said. "He's going Hollywood already? Maybe he thinks he's, like, a big-time rapper or something."

"And he doesn't just have *one* entourage," Hunter said. "He's got *three!*"

The rest of the Orioles turned to stare at him.

"Nerd, do you even know what an entourage *is*?" Katelyn said. "Do yourself a favor, okay? Look it up before you try to use it in a sentence."

As everyone cracked up, Zoom slowly made his way to the dugout while his three buddies and his dad clambered up into the stands. Zoom nodded to Coach, who was standing near the entrance, ready to fill out the lineup card.

Then the pitcher threw his bag on the bench and fished out his glove and some sunflower seeds.

Uh-oh, Mickey thought, this won't go over well with Dad.

No, his dad was an absolute fanatic about his players arriving on time for everything—practices, games, any kind of team function. If a kid was even a few minutes late, Coach would pointedly remind him or her—usually in a voice loud enough to be heard in Montana—of the team rules about punctuality.

And if the kid was ever late again—*BOOM!*—that was it. The miscreant would be on the bench for the next game— and maybe for the game after that, too.

Coach wasn't afraid to get on the kid's mom or dad, either, if the problem was the parent not getting the kid to a ball game on time.

But showing up just fifteen minutes before first pitch? Oh, Dad's gonna go thermonuclear, Mickey thought. No doubt about it: he's gonna blow.

Except . . . he didn't.

Mickey was shocked to see a smile cross his dad's face when he spotted Zoom.

"Hey, big guy, glad you made it!" his dad said, sounding relieved. "Great day for a ball game, isn't it? You're gonna pitch lights-out for us—I can feel it! Now you and Mickey go warm up."

Mickey stared incredulously at his dad, wondering if some alien life-form had taken over his body.

What? his dad said, noticing the look. Then, in a stern voice, "C'mon, Mick! It's almost game time. You gonna help Zoom get loose or what?"

Mickey shook his head and said, "Sure, Dad. Whatever you say."

He grabbed his mitt and motioned for Zoom to follow. Together they went down the right-field line, where a practice mound and plate were set up.

But as soon as Mickey crouched behind the plate, Zoom held up his hands.

"Whoa!" he said, waving his arms. "I can't just start . . . *throwing*."

"You can't?" Mickey said. "And why is that?"

Zoom snorted.

"Are you serious, dude?" He held up his right arm. "This could be a million-dollar arm someday! I gotta protect this baby. Gotta do some stretching first."

Well, Mickey thought, that didn't take long. The kid's been here for, what, two minutes? And he's already ticking off people.

Namely me.

"We already did stretching—as a *team*," Mickey said testily. "About fifty minutes ago. Which is when we were all supposed to be here, remember?"

But Zoom wasn't listening. He was already contorting his body into an elaborate pose, teetering on one foot with the other leg tucked behind it, his right arm reaching behind his head to touch his left shoulder blade.

He looks like a drunken flamingo, Mickey thought. But he said nothing else as Zoom continued to stretch. Finally, Zoom picked up his glove and a ball and nodded. "Okay, big man, let's do this," he said.

Zoom was a model of quiet efficiency warming up—Mickey had to give him that. The boy needed only ten pitches before he pronounced himself loose. He threw six sizzling fastballs, two changeups, and two curves. Every one of them seemed to track Mickey's mitt from the moment they left Zoom's hand.

If he throws like that in the game, Mickey thought, the Blue Jays are in huge trouble. And the game will be over in an hour. On the other hand, Mickey had seen plenty of pitchers who looked great in warm-ups and then got shelled or walked ten batters when the game started.

Let's see how Mr. Elite Arms does when it counts, he thought.

They returned to the dugout and Mickey grunted to his dad, "He's ready." Then, turning to Zoom, he said, "Okay, let's go over the signs."

Zoom's face clouded over.

"Didn't we already have this discussion?" he said. "We don't need signs. I'm throwing mostly heat. If I'm gonna mix in a curveball, I'll do this."

He stuck his tongue out of the side of his mouth. It reminded Mickey of the old videos he'd seen of Michael Jordan swooping into the lane for a dunk with his tongue flapping.

"And if it's a changeup coming," Zoom continued, "I'll do this."

This time he closed his eyes for an instant as he pretended to go into his windup.

Mickey looked at his dad. He was one of the few coaches

in the league who still let the catcher call pitches. Most of the other coaches had turned into massive control freaks who insisted on calling pitches from the dugout.

Maybe they thought it made them look cool, relaying signs the way Buck Showalter, Joe Girardi, and other big-league managers and pitching coaches did. Or maybe they were trying to impress the parents in the stands and make it appear like they were orchestrating the game, on top of every little detail.

But relaying a sign from the coach to the catcher and then to the pitcher took way too long and made every at-bat drag. Besides, Mickey's dad had always felt the game—especially at this level—belonged to the kids who played it. He wasn't going to start micromanaging pitch selections for his team.

Not only that, but he had always trusted Mickey's judgment in calling pitches. "Who knows more about the hitters in this league than the Mick?" his dad often said.

But now Mickey could see his dad wavering. Coach looked from one boy to the other, licking his lips nervously.

"Let Zoom throw what he wants," he said finally. "What's the big deal? If it makes him comfortable the first time out for us . . ."

But Mickey was already shaking his head and walking to the far end of the dugout. Thanks, Dad, he thought. Way to totally cave to the new kid. And stick the knife in your son's back.

Oh, and good luck having a pitcher—no matter what kind of a hotshot he's supposed to be—throwing whatever he wants to hitters he's never seen in a league as good as this one.

And another thing: how dumb did Zoom think the Blue Jays were? It would take them maybe five seconds to pick up on that stupid tongue sign. And maybe seven seconds to see that closed eyes equals a big, fat changeup that they could hit into the next area code.

Mickey was still fuming when the Orioles took the field and the first Blue Jays batter stepped in.

From atop the mound, Zoom smirked at the kid and went into his windup.

Would I be a horrible human being, Mickey wondered, if I rooted for this kid to jack the first pitch over the center-field fence?

But the only thing the batter hit was air.

Instead of smacking a titanic homer and following it with a triumphant trot around the bases, the kid waved at three straight fastballs and shuffled back to the dugout.

All Zoom did after that was strike out the side.

On eleven pitches, total.

The Blue Jays number two hitter actually managed to foul off a pitch. And the next batter looked at a pitch that was maybe an inch outside for a ball.

Otherwise it was one futile swing or called strike after another for the Jays as Zoom overpowered them with his stuff. After the third kid whiffed to end the inning, Mickey stole a glance at the Jays dugout and saw players looking wide-eyed at one another, as if to say, *Okay, who's this beast? And where did he come from?*

"Anyone time that inning?" Katelyn said as the Orioles ran off the field. "Might be the quickest one in the history of organized baseball."

Zoom took a seat at the end of the bench. One by one the Orioles went by to tap him on the knee or give him a fist bump and say, "Good job," with Zoom grunting his thanks.

Grudgingly, Mickey joined the receiving line to the new pitcher.

"That was some start," Mickey said when he reached him. "Keep it up."

"Don't have to worry about that," Zoom said. "Just sit back and give me a target, big guy. I'll do the rest."

I'm sure you will, Mickey thought. Guess the rest of the team can pretty much pack up and go home, right?

The Orioles failed to score in their half of the inning and Zoom was soon back on the mound. This time he was almost as quick in dispensing with the Jays, striking out their cleanup and number five hitters before allowing a weak ground ball to third, which Hunter gobbled up for the final out.

"Hey, Zoom, you gotta do better than that," Hunter said playfully when the O's were back in the dugout. "I almost broke a sweat on that last grounder. Had to move a whole two feet to my left."

"My bad," Zoom said.

The rest of the Orioles grinned. But looking at Zoom, they quickly realized he was dead serious.

In fact, he was fuming.

"That kid goes down on three pitches next time he's up," Zoom growled. "That's a promise."

The Orioles looked at one another and shook their heads.

"Hey, nerd—lighten up!" Katelyn shouted to Zoom. "Hunter was just being facetious."

"Yeah," Hunter said. "I was just being fa—um, you know, whatever she said."

Mickey was up, so he grabbed his bat and tuned out the rest of the conversation. He needed to concentrate. If he couldn't help the team behind the plate with his signal calling, maybe he could get things going for the Orioles at the plate.

The Blue Jays pitcher was a skinny, nervous-looking kid named Jeremy Pruitt, who was known to blink furiously the minute he took the mound. The Orioles had faced him twice last season and they quickly nicknamed him the Mole.

As he stepped in against him, Mickey remembered that there was another key piece of info about the Mole floating somewhere in his brain. His dad always said that Mickey was a veritable database about every player the Orioles had ever faced.

But now Mickey was drawing a blank. Whatever snippet of intel he had on the Mole was rattling around somewhere in his cranium, but Mickey was at a loss to corral it.

Think, he admonished himself. *Think!*

Finally it came to him: the kid throws a wicked changeup. Yes, that's it! The Mole has one of the best changeups in the league. Only he relies on it way too much. He'll throw it every three or four pitches instead of waiting until the batter's so amped up for a fastball that he'll practically screw himself into the ground on an off-speed pitch.

Wait for the changeup, Mickey told himself. It'll come. Big and fat and shiny, like the best present you ever unwrapped on a Christmas morning.

This time it came on a 1-and-1 count.

Mickey was ready for it.

He kept his weight back until the last second and

uncoiled his hips and shoulder smoothly, hitting a shot that soared toward the flagpole in left center field and cleared the fence by ten feet. As he circled the bases and slapped hands with his dad, the rest of the Orioles gathered on the top step of the dugout, whooping and cheering.

Even Zoom, Mickey noticed, was on his feet clapping, although he looked about as happy as a kid whose dog had just been run over.

It was the spark the Orioles needed.

Corey followed with a double down the left-field line. First baseman Ethan Novitsky drove him in with a sharp single up the middle, and Justin Pryor, the O's second base-man, followed with a run-scoring double to right.

Just like that, the Orioles led 3–0. Which meant Zoom had a comfortable cushion with which to work.

Not that he needed it.

He struck out the first batter in the top of the third and got the next batter on a slow roller to Justin at second. The next kid managed a checked-swing blooper over Ethan's head that dribbled down the right-field line for a base hit, which caused the Jays dugout to erupt like he'd just hit a grand-slam homer.

But Zoom quickly struck out the next kid to end the inning.

Back in the dugout, though, the Orioles were still snort-ing over the Blue Jays' lucky hit and the wild celebration it had touched off.

"Please! Don't they realize the kid was just trying to get out of the way of a nasty curveball?" Sammy said. "And that he just happened to stick his bat out?"

"I'm surprised they weren't spraying champagne all over each other," Katelyn said. "All over a dinky little nothing swing."

She stood and cupped her hands around her mouth and yelled out to the Blue Jays, "Hey, nerds! Get a clue on that weak hit! Not exactly a Chris Davis moon shot!"

It quickly earned her a death stare from Coach. But Katelyn pretended not to notice him as she sat down with a self-satisfied smile.

The Blue Jays did no better in the fourth inning against Zoom, who set them down one, two, three. A minute or so later, Gabe sat down next to Mickey at the end of the bench.

"Dude," he whispered, "this Zoom kid is pitching lights-out."

Mickey nodded.

"No, I mean *really* lights-out," Gabe said. "He's scary good."

"I know," Mickey said wearily. "I didn't move the glove two inches all game. You could catch for him while sitting on a lawn chair if you wanted to."

When Coach brought Danny in to pitch the final two innings, Zoom's stat line was positively glittering: four innings pitched, one hit, six strikeouts, zero walks.

Danny gave up a couple of hits but otherwise performed solidly, and the Orioles held on for a 3–0 win. Still, there was something gnawing at Mickey as the two teams lined up to slap hands.

Yes, Zoom had looked All-World, exactly as advertised— well, exactly as *he'd* advertised himself, anyway.

He seemed every inch the wonder boy who had lit up

the Elite Arms Camp, the kid with the rifle arm and limitless future who seemed heaven-sent to help the Orioles make a run for the playoffs.

Not only that, but Mickey's dad had been practically giddy with excitement after the game, hugging Zoom and high-fiving the rest of the O's as if they'd just won some big-deal championship.

Then why, Mickey wondered, wasn't he happier?

Why didn't this win feel as satisfying as all the others? It wasn't as if he himself had played a bad game. Sure, he hadn't been as involved in the game due to not calling pitches—through, ahem, no fault of his own.

But hadn't he hit his fifth homer of the season, a tape-measure job into a stiff breeze that ignited the Orioles rally, a shot that felt better than any other he'd hit all season?

Then what was the *problem*?

He was still trying to figure it out as he threw his gear into his bag and headed slowly out to his dad's truck in the parking lot.

As he passed the snowball stand on the edge of the field, he heard a rustle of movement inside.

Out of the corner of his eye, he saw a flash of long brown hair as someone leaned over the counter.

Then a girl's voice said, "Boy, you look awful, you know that? What you need is one of Abby's famous frozen concoctions. It's a little slice of heaven. And all it costs is a dollar."

Now the voice took on an edge.

"Oh, and please don't tell me you don't have a dollar. Because I swear, I will leap over this counter and come out there and pound you."

7

Mickey found himself staring into the greenest eyes he had ever seen. And they were twinkling. The girl stood in front of a silver ice-shaving machine. On the shelves behind her were stacks of paper cups and row after row of multicolored syrup bottles that seemed to glow in the last rays of the setting sun.

"Is that really a sound business practice?" he asked. "Threatening customers with a beatdown if they don't stop and buy something?"

She crossed her arms and seemed amused.

"You'd be surprised at how well it works," she said. "Anyway, I only do it when sales are slow. Otherwise I turn on the charm. Like this."

She batted her eyelashes and said in a high-pitched voice, "Thanks so much, y'all, for helping a poor, struggling, seventh-grade entrepreneur with the purchase of one of these delectable summertime treats!"

Mickey laughed and studied the sign on the wall that read:

ABBY ELLIOTT, SNOWBALL MAKER TO THE STARS

"You're new around here, right?" he said. "Hate to tell you, you won't find too many stars at this field."

"Oh, I don't know," she said. "Your name's Mickey, right? They say you're the best catcher in the league. So you're a star. Then there's that new kid on your team, Zoom? I watched him hammer those Blue Jays tonight. What an arm! That kid is *definitely* a star!"

Mickey groaned and fished a rumpled dollar bill from his uniform pants.

"Can we not discuss him right now?" he said.

"Oh, touchy subject, eh?" Abby said. "Okay, we'll move on. What flavor do you want, star?"

"Grape, please."

Abby rolled her eyes. She pretended to stifle a yawn.

"Gee, *grape!*" she said. "There's a bold move! No one *ever* gets grape! Way to push the envelope! Way to think outside the box!"

She reached over the counter and grabbed his arm.

"Have you checked the calendar lately? It's 2015, star. They have all sorts of new flavors now: banana cream pie, peach melba, York Peppermint Pattie. Try one! Go wild!"

Mickey pulled his arm back and grinned.

"Maybe you're right," he said. "Maybe I *do* have to broaden my horizons. Okay, make it grape—with marshmallow topping."

Abby threw up her hands in surrender.

"Fine," she said. She reached for a paper cup and filled it with shaved ice. "I run into your type all the time. A traditionalist. Old-school to the core. Have it your way. One grape with marshmallow coming up."

She pivoted gracefully and grabbed a bottle of syrup from the second shelf. Carefully she layered the sticky purple liquid throughout the ice before stabbing it with a plastic spoon and sliding it across the counter.

"There's an art form to making a snowball," she said. "People think there's nothing to it. But you need the perfect ratio of syrup to ice. Otherwise, know what you've got?"

Mickey shook his head.

"YOU'VE GOT A BIG MUSHY MESS THAT TASTES HORRIBLE!" Abby roared. She pointed at Mickey's snowball. "Now look at that baby right there. I don't want to sound like I'm bragging, but presentation-wise, that belongs on a magazine cover. Or behind glass in a museum. Go ahead, taste it."

Mickey took a giant spoonful. He was surprised at how hot and thirsty he was. Then again, he couldn't ever remember a time when he wasn't hot and thirsty after catching six innings in all that gear.

"Mmmm, it's really great," he said, crunching the ice. "Very tasty and refreshing and—"

Abby held up a hand.

"Okay, fine, don't strain yourself with the adjectives. But it's delicious, right? Delicious to the nth power. The best snowball you ever had in your entire life. No, go ahead and say it. You wouldn't be the first person."

Mickey nodded. "You might as well call this place 'World's Greatest Snowballs.'" He watched her face light up and said, "You really love this job, don't you?"

"Absolutely," she said. "I get to make people happy. Who *doesn't* love snowballs? And who doesn't smile when you hand them one?"

"Even when you threaten to pound them first?" Mickey asked.

"Even then," Abby said with a smile. "A well-made snowball makes up for everything. Even bad first impressions."

Suddenly she grew serious.

"On the other hand," she said, "the job is not without its occupational hazards."

Mickey snickered. "Like what? Tooth decay from all the sugar in these things?"

"No, it's not that," Abby said. She looked around nervously and whispered, "Bees."

"Probably don't have to whisper," Mickey said. "I don't think they can understand you."

"The syrup drives bees crazy," Abby continued. "They're not around just yet. It's a little early in the season. But when they get here, look out. The owner says she had three workers stung last summer. And a few customers, too."

She sighed. "Kids crying and screaming at a snowball stand—not real great for business, as you can imagine."

She wiped down the counter with a damp cloth and smiled again.

"But there are so many good things about the job," she said. "Like, when I don't have any customers, I get to watch baseball. I play softball, but baseball's my favorite sport in the whole world. In fact, I got to watch most of your game tonight."

Mickey shrugged. "Decent game, I guess. We won. End of story."

"Oh, I can see you're absolutely giddy with excitement," Abby said drily. "Didn't you hit a huge home run to put your team ahead? And didn't Zoom kill the Jays with four innings of shutout ball? And didn't your team get one step closer to the playoffs?" She frowned. "So what's with the 'eh' reaction, star?"

"It's a long story," Mickey said, draining the last of his snowball.

She stared at him for a moment before nodding thoughtfully.

"Okay," she said, "it *did* seem like something wasn't quite right with you guys tonight. Look, I'm a snowball mixologist, not a sports psychologist. But the team chemistry definitely seemed to be . . . off. And I think I know the problem."

"You do, huh?" Mickey said, leaning forward. "And what exactly is that?"

She looked at her watch. "Can't go into it tonight," she said. "Have to close up. And you have to go. Isn't that your dad out there beeping the horn?"

It was dusk and the parking lot was mostly empty now. Mickey turned to see his dad waving and flashing the truck's headlights.

"To be continued," he said. He slung his gear bag over his shoulders and waved before jogging off.

"You know where to find me, star!" Abby called after him. "And next time, let's try expanding that palate of yours. No more grape, okay? There's a whole new world of flavor out there! Live a little!"

From his seat behind home plate at Camden Yards, Mickey watched the New York Yankees' Jacoby Ellsbury take his lead off first base.

Ellsbury's eyes were twin lasers locked on the pitcher. His fingers were twitching nervously. His feet were doing this miniature tap dance, kicking up tiny clouds of dust with his cleats, the telltale sign of a runner who wants to go.

In the next instant, he broke for second.

Dead meat, Mickey thought.

Matt Wieters, the great Baltimore Orioles catcher, lunged for the outside pitch, set his feet quickly, and fired a perfect strike to second base. J. J. Hardy, the shortstop, barely had to move his glove to make the tag.

The umpire waved a fist in the air like he was going to punch someone and shouted, "HE'S OUT!"

An unholy roar rose from the stands.

"Told you," Mickey whispered as Ellsbury trotted back to the dugout with his head down.

Dead meat.

It was two days after the Blue Jays game, and Mickey and his dad were among the sellout crowd at the Yards for the start of the big weekend series between the Orioles and Yankees.

Mickey loved it when his father got tickets here in section 36, because it gave him a great close-up look at the catchers of both teams. And there was no catcher he enjoyed studying more than Wieters, the O's three-time All-Star, who was no more than fifteen feet from them on the other side of the protective screen.

"Look at him," his dad said, shaking his head in wonder. "He's six-foot-five and two hundred and forty pounds. Can you believe that? He's the size of an NFL tight end! Probably the strongest catcher in the game. And he moves like a ballet dancer."

Mickey nodded, his gaze never leaving Wieters.

"And the arm!" his dad continued. "The guy's an absolute freak! Plus no one gets rid of the ball quicker. His transfer from the glove to his throwing hand is ridiculous."

His dad was starting to sound like Wieters's agent, but Mickey agreed with that assessment, too.

Just one inning earlier, Wieters had pulled off a similarly dazzling fielding gem. Brett Gardner, the Yankees speedy outfielder, had laid down what seemed to be a perfect bunt, pushing it into the no-man's-land between the pitcher's mound and home plate.

Chris Tillman, the Orioles pitcher, had frozen momentarily, wondering if it was his play or his catcher's. But Wieters hadn't frozen. In a flash, the big catcher had whipped off his mask and pounced on the ball, scooping it in his mitt with a sweeping motion.

Then he had pirouetted and fired a dart to first base that had beaten Gardner by three feet as the Orioles fans howled with approval.

Thinking about both of those great plays, Mickey wondered: How much of that was Matt Wieters's natural talent? And how much was hard work and dedication and all those other things that gym teachers and coaches and the ex-jocks on ESPN were always talking about?

When Matt Wieters was a kid, did he do crazy stuff like invite a friend over on a ninety-degree day to throw balls at him and smash up his garage door just so he could practice blocking pitches?

Maybe so, Mickey thought.

It would be awesome to hear that someday.

Or maybe young Matt Wieters had relied on a different set of drills to hone his . . . but now Mickey became dimly aware of his father's voice cutting through the crowd noise.

"Did you hear me, Mick?" his dad was saying. "I was asking if anything was bothering you. You've been really quiet all night."

As a matter of fact, Mickey thought, something *is* bothering me. *Really* bothering me. He'd been thinking about it so much, his head felt like it was going to explode. But was this really the time and place to talk about it?

Sure, he'd been looking for the right moment to sit down with his dad for the past two days. But his dad had worked late every night and come home too exhausted for any serious discussions.

Now, here in the middle of a packed stadium, with the Orioles playing their hated divisional rivals in a close game, and the noise level reaching that of a 747 at takeoff, and the usual "YANKEES SUCK!" chants erupting every five minutes, was this really the place to—

"It's about Zoom, isn't it?" his dad said.

As upset as he was with his dad, Mickey had to suppress a smile. *Unreal!* Sometimes it was as if his dad was some kind of mind reader, or all-knowing, all-seeing Eastern mystic. Especially when something was troubling his only child.

"Go ahead, get it off your chest," his dad continued. "You'll feel better. Then I'll feel better. *Maybe.*"

The Orioles were hustling off the field. It was the middle of the fourth inning and the giant scoreboard screen in center field was flashing a crowd favorite: the Esskay Hot Dog Race around the bases between Mustard, Ketchup, and Relish.

Normally Mickey liked watching these silly races—this time the cartoon figures were astride a horse, a kangaroo, and a rhinoceros. As always, he rooted for Ketchup, the King of the Condiments, which made him think of the burger and fries he had polished off in the second inning.

But he sensed his dad was not going to let this issue drop.

"Okay," Mickey said. "Why didn't you say anything to Zoom when he was late for the game?"

At first, his dad looked puzzled. Then he looked annoyed.

"Really?" he said. "*Seriously? That's* why you're upset? Because I didn't jump the new kid for being a few minutes late?"

"Forty-five minutes late, to be exact," Mickey said, suddenly sorry he had said anything. "You get on everyone else if they're five minutes late."

His dad stared at him. Mickey stole a glance at the scoreboard. Ketchup was winning by the length of the kangaroo's tail as they rounded first base. "Go, Ketchup!" he whispered.

Right now he wished he were up on the screen with the happy racing figures instead of here under his dad's withering gaze.

"Not a big issue," his dad snapped. "I cut Zoom some slack, okay? Let it go. What else has you all mopey? Might as well get it all out now."

Ohhh-kay, we're off to a great start here, Mickey thought. Do I really want to bring up the second thing that's bothering me? Sure, why not? How could things get worse?

He took a deep breath. *And the kid swings for the fences . . .*

"You also let Zoom call his own pitches," he began. "I've called the pitches for two years for the Orioles. And we've done pretty well . . ."

His dad waved a hand dismissively.

"If that's what makes the boy comfortable his first time out for us, what's the harm?" he said. "Sometimes you have to take one for the team, Mick. It can't always be about you. I thought you understood that. But I can see I was wrong.

"We needed a good outing from Zoom and we got one," his dad continued. "Don't you want to win the league this year? Huh? Now we're another step closer. Isn't that what we're all trying to accomplish?"

Mickey started to say something. But his dad's jaw was set and his arms were crossed and he'd turned his attention back to the game.

It was classic Dad Body Language. And what it said was: This discussion is over.

Period, end of story.

Mickey sighed. *Thanks, Dad. Good talk. Really made me feel better.*

He looked up at the scoreboard and saw that Mustard was winning as the three condiments headed for third. But his thoughts quickly turned back to Zach and the special treatment his dad had given the kid from the very beginning.

Mickey had never seen his dad act that way toward anyone before. Maybe this was the "human nature" his dad was always talking about.

Didn't teachers fawn over the smart kids in their classes—the ones who shot their hands in the air all the time and always knew the answers and seemed so *interested*? Didn't teachers reward those kids with smiles and compliments?

And didn't those same teachers sometimes look at other students—the kids who struggled in class, and especially the out-and-out dumb ones—as if they'd just tracked in dog poop?

Sure they did.

And it wasn't only in class where Mickey had witnessed kids being treated differently.

Mickey had seen coaches on his Pop Warner football teams and rec-league basketball teams look the other way when their best players acted up in practice and disrupted drills.

As long as they were rushing for a hundred yards or making twenty tackles, as long as they were scoring twenty points a game in hoops or pulling down a dozen rebounds, they could get away with anything.

No, Mickey thought, the superstars were always getting breaks, no matter the venue. And Zach had sure looked like a superstar against the Blue Jays. There was no arguing that.

He heard another roar from the crowd and looked up. On the scoreboard, a triumphant-looking Ketchup had just crossed home plate to win the race. His trusty kangaroo had even launched into an awesome hook slide to beat Relish by a hair.

Mickey pumped his fist and whispered, "Yes-s-s!"

Once again, Ketchup was a superstar, too.

Which—big surprise—made Mickey hungry all over again.

As upset as he was, Mickey could always eat.

Mickey wondered if he'd entered some parallel universe where nothing ever changes. Because what was happening now was almost spooky.

It felt like that old movie he'd once watched with his parents, *Groundhog Day*, about the weatherman who lives the same day over and over.

Here he was at Eddie Murray Field, crouched behind the plate on another hot summer night with a scowling Zoom on the mound—again.

And Zoom was mowing down the opposing batters with ease—again.

And calling his own pitches—again—thanks to yet another monumental cave-in by Mickey's dad, who seemed incapable of denying any of the wishes of his new hard-throwing pitcher.

Not only that, but the Orioles were up 3–0—again.

The only difference this time was that they were playing the Red Sox, one of the best teams in the league, instead of the sad-sack Blue Jays.

Actually, there was one other difference. Zoom had

been only half an hour late for this game, his dad's SUV disgorging him and the same solemn three-kid entourage just after the Orioles had finished taking the infield.

Once again, the team had reacted with amazement when Mickey's dad said nothing after Zoom sauntered into the dugout so late.

"Dude, what's the deal with Coach?" Gabe had whispered to Mickey. "Is this the same coach who killed me for being late to the Queen City Tournament last month?"

"And tore me up for coming ten minutes late for practice?" Sammy said. "Now the new guy shows up whenever he wants? *Seriously?*"

Mickey had shrugged and said nothing.

What was there to say? He couldn't figure out what was going on with his dad, either. It got even more mystifying right before game time, when his dad took him aside and murmured, "Hey, buddy, just let Zoom throw whatever he wants again. And don't make a big deal out of it, okay? This'll probably be the last time we let him do it."

Sure, Dad, Mickey thought. Next time you'll *really* crack the whip, right?

Now here was Mickey in the second inning, trying to stay focused behind the plate. He had singled in a run in his first at-bat and scored on Spencer's two-run double. But without the added stimulation of calling pitches and being really engaged in the field, and with Zoom overpowering one batter after another, he found his mind wandering.

With two outs, a skinny, nervous kid who looked like he couldn't hit the ball past the pitcher's mound was up for the Red Sox.

Great, Mickey thought. For the first time in his life, he wondered if you could actually fall asleep from sheer boredom in the middle of a baseball game.

Suddenly Zoom raised his hands and called for time. He waved for Mickey to join him for a conference. He motioned for the entire infield to join them, too.

"We're going to walk this guy," he said when everyone had gathered.

"Ex-*cuse* me?" Hunter said. "Why exactly would we do that?"

"So I can pick him off," Zoom said.

"So you can . . . *what?!*"

Sammy glanced back at the batter, who was taking a practice cut and gripping the bat so tightly his knuckles were white.

"He looks terrified, Z," Sammy said. "Why not just sit his butt down on three fastballs?"

"More fun this way," Zoom said with a wink. "Besides, you guys have never seen my pickoff move."

Mickey felt his anger rising.

"Send us a video," he barked. "We don't want to see your pickoff move now. We're trying to win a game here. And we're not taking any stupid chances."

"I'm telling you, big man, my pickoff is money," Zoom said. "Voted the best one at the Elite Arms Camp."

Sammy rolled his eyes and sighed.

"Here we go again with the Elite Arms stuff," he said. "Ever get tired of bringing that up? Would it be possible for you to go, like, one game without mentioning it?"

The umpire walked to the mound and shouted, "Let's go, guys! I'd like to be home before the eleven o'clock news, okay?"

"Yes, sir, Mr. Ump!" Zoom said, snapping off a sarcastic salute. Then he murmured to the Orioles, "Everybody stay loose. Watch the master at work."

As Mickey jogged back to the plate, his dad shouted from the dugout, "What was that all about?"

Mickey just shrugged. You'll find out soon enough, he thought.

Now Zoom, who had shown pinpoint control all night, suddenly seemed to lose it. Ball one was two feet outside. Mickey had to lunge to backhand it. The next pitch was even farther outside. The kid never took the bat off his shoulder. The next two pitches were in the dirt.

Looking enormously relieved, the kid tossed his bat aside and trotted down to first base, high-fiving the Red Sox assistant coach. Zoom watched with a smirk. A moment later, as the kid took his lead off first, Zoom went into the stretch and nodded knowingly to Mickey.

No-o-o-o, Mickey thought. He's going to try a pickoff without even throwing a pitch?

Which was exactly what Zoom was thinking.

Seemingly in one motion, he stepped off the pitching rubber, whirled, and threw to first. The Red Sox runner was frozen. Now he was five feet off the bag and scrambling to get back, his feet spinning frantically in the loose dirt like Wile E. Coyote in a Road Runner cartoon trying not to go barreling off a cliff.

Dead meat, Mickey thought.

Deader than Jacoby Ellsbury the other night.

Mickey had to admit it: that jerk Zoom was right. He *did* have a sweet pickoff move—even if this was no way to break it out.

Except . . . Zoom's throw sailed over Ethan's head. The big first baseman chased the ball down as it slammed off the fence and bounded down the right-field line. By the time Katelyn finally retrieved it and fired a one-hopper to the plate, the runner was sliding in ahead of Mickey's sweep tag.

Orioles 3, Red Sox 1.

Just like that, the Red Sox were back in the game. What was once an intimidated, dispirited team was now up and whooping in the dugout.

Mickey turned to look at Zoom, who'd been backing up home on the play.

Zoom shrugged and flashed a sheepish grin.

"Oh, well," he said. "So much for that idea."

Mickey was furious now. He started to say something, then shook his head and turned away.

Zoom settled down and struck out the next batter on four pitches to end the inning. But when Mickey jogged back to the dugout, his dad was waiting for him on the top step. He didn't look happy.

"What in God's name happened out there?" he asked. "One minute Zoom's on cruise control, the next we're throwing the ball all over the place. You're the catcher! You're supposed to be showing leadership out there. Instead you guys looked awful!"

You guys? Mickey thought.

He brushed past his dad, sat down, and slammed his mitt on the floor.

"Better ask your new pitcher what happened," he snapped. "He's got all the answers."

Mickey hated snitches. Tattletales, rats,

squealers—whatever you called them, he couldn't stand
them.

He was steaming, angrier than he'd ever been on a baseball field. And all because of the most selfish, egotistical
kid he'd ever seen in his life.

But if his dad wanted details about the pickoff fiasco
and how a jittery batter who looked like he'd blow over in
a stiff breeze somehow managed to get on base and score
against a shutdown pitcher like Zoom, he'd have to get
them from someone else.

And apparently his dad *did* want details.

"Zoom," Coach said in a low voice, "step into my office
for a moment."

The two left the dugout and leaned against the chain-
link fence a few feet away. The rest of the Orioles couldn't
hear what was being said. But they could see Coach listening intently, his arms folded across his chest as Zoom
delivered an animated explanation.

When they returned, Zoom wore a smug look. And Coach was smiling.

Unreal, Mickey thought. Can't wait to hear how Zoom spins this one.

He didn't have to wait long.

A moment later, as he leaned over to loosen his shin guards, he felt a beefy hand on his back.

"Sounds like Zoom just lost his control for a moment," his dad said. "It happens. And Ethan probably should have caught the pickoff throw, right? Anyway, no biggie. We move on."

Mickey's jaw dropped. He stared at his dad to see if this was some sort of joke.

Lost his control? Really? And he was blaming Ethan for the throw? When everyone on the field knew Shaquille O'Neal couldn't have caught that ball if he were standing on a stepladder? And holding a butterfly net?

Mickey glanced at Zoom, who grinned. Then Zoom clamped a batting helmet on his head and headed out to the on-deck circle.

"Uh, that's not exactly what happened—" Mickey started to say. But his dad was already jogging out to the third-base coach's box with the Orioles coming to bat.

So apparently this discussion was over, too.

Great, he thought. Another good talk, Dad.

This time he grabbed his water bottle and fired it against the far wall.

"Whoa! Someone better work on his anger issues," Gabe said, plopping down next to him. "Catcher's mitt, water bottle—you're two-for-two with the meltdowns."

Mickey shook his head, but said nothing.

"Deep breaths, dude," Gabe said, watching Zoom dig in at the plate now. "Don't let that guy get to you."

"Too late," Mickey said between clenched teeth. "He got to me the first time I saw him."

The Orioles padded their lead when Zoom hit a double down the left-field line and scored on Hunter's single. One batter later, Katelyn smacked a towering home run over the right-field fence: 6–1 Orioles.

They were still high-fiving one another in the dugout when a clamor arose from the stands. Katelyn ran to the edge of the steps and peered out.

"Oh, you gotta see this!" she said. "Check out Tweedledee, Tweedledumb, and Tweedledumber."

Mickey, Gabe, and Hunter hurried over and followed her gaze. There, at the top of the bleachers, was Zoom's entourage. Only now the three boys were laughing uproariously and high-fiving one another.

"They actually show emotion?" Gabe said. "I thought they were robots. You know, like if you tore their shirts off and drilled a hole in their backs, you'd find a mass of wires and circuits instead of flesh and blood."

"Keep watching, it gets better," Katelyn said. "They're doing a three-man wave! And I use the term *three man* loosely. It's more like a three-dork wave."

As if on cue, the boys sprang into action. One by one they leaped to their feet, threw their hands in the air, and shouted, "Wooooo!"

"I'm sorry," Hunter said, "but that's just *wrong*."

"On so many levels," Katelyn added.

The rest of the spectators were watching this strange show, too. Even the home-plate umpire was swiveling his neck between pitches to see what was happening.

Katelyn called down to the end of the bench, "Hey, Zoom, check it out! Your boys are going mental in the stands."

With a puzzled look, Zoom sauntered over and peered up at the commotion. His face clouded. He put two fingers to his lips and delivered a piercing whistle.

When the boys looked over, Zoom made a quick slicing motion across his throat, the universal sign for *Cut it out!*

Immediately, the three sat down, looking chastened.

"Oooooh!" Hunter said. "Way to have major control over your peeps, Zoom!"

Zoom nodded with a satisfied smile. He sat back down without a word as the Orioles looked at one another.

"Wow, that was weird," Sammy whispered.

"Oh, yeah," Katelyn said. "Wonder if his dogs are that well trained."

The rest of the game seemed to go by quickly. The Orioles added two more runs in the fourth, and Danny pitched the last three innings, allowing just two hits and one run to seal the 8–2 win.

As the two teams lined up to slap hands, Mickey did the math.

Three more wins and they'd have a shot at the league title. Which, of course, meant a shot at knocking off the Evil Empire, the powerful Huntington Yankees, who were— surprise!—undefeated and running away with their league championship again.

But once again, he didn't feel like celebrating. All he

knew at the moment was that he was hot and tired. And maybe for the first time in his life, he was happy the game was over.

Maybe a snowball will help, Mickey thought. And the truth was, it wouldn't hurt to see Abby again. It had been fun talking to her last week. Any girl that threatened to clock you for not buying her product was definitely, well, interesting.

Mickey had to admit he'd thought of Abby often since that first meeting, even though between school and sports and his friends, he really didn't have time for girls.

Not that a kid's priorities couldn't change at some point, he told himself.

As he walked toward the snowball stand a few minutes later, he could see that it was busy. Six or seven kids were scattered around the picnic tables out front, enjoying their frozen treats and the last warm rays of the sun.

As he rounded the corner, he saw that Abby was talking to someone at the counter. The person was obscured by the big cardboard floor sign that listed the flavors and prices. All Mickey could see was that Abby had her head thrown back and was laughing loudly, as if whatever she'd just heard was the funniest thing in the whole world.

Whoever was behind the sign took a step back and Mickey saw a sliver of an orange-and-black jersey and white uniform pants. Then a breeze blew the sign back and the mystery customer was revealed.

It was Zoom.

Mickey groaned. Just who I want to see . . .

When Abby looked up and saw Mickey, she smiled and waved.

"Look at this!" she said. "Two stars gracing my humble place of employment at the same time! Is this my lucky day or what?"

Zoom didn't seem nearly as thrilled with the interruption.

"Well, if it isn't my catcher," he said in a loud voice. He walked up to Mickey and poked an index finger in his belly.

"Honest opinion, big man?" he said. "Forget the snowball. What you need is a salad, dude. With low-fat dressing."

Abby gasped. Mickey felt his face get hot. From somewhere behind him, he heard guffaws. He turned and saw Zoom's three buddies cracking up at one of the picnic tables.

Mickey slapped Zoom's finger away and took a step toward him. Just then a car horn sounded and Zoom's dad pulled up to the curb.

"Hate to eat and run, but what can you do?" Zoom said with a smirk. He spooned the last of his snowball, nodded to his buddies, and the four of them strutted away.

As Abby watched them leave, she said, "Okay, now I'm *really* beginning to sense a problem with your team . . ."

Mickey nodded slowly.

"Oh," he said, "you have no idea."

Augie's House of Wings was filling up, the mostly young crowd drawn by the weekly all-you-can-eat special.

A group of Orioles had walked to the restaurant after practice. They sat at a table in the back, studying Mickey with a combination of awe and alarm.

In front of the big catcher were two plates. One held a steaming heap of buffalo wings glistening with Augie's secret sauce, a spicy, iridescent orange glaze. The other plate held at least fifty chicken bones, gnawed clean as if by a wild animal.

When he finished devouring each wing, Mickey dropped it on the plate—where it landed with a distinctive *ping*—while he simultaneously reached for another.

The time between the final slurp of a devoured wing and a meaty new one reaching his lips was estimated to be two seconds by the rest of the Orioles.

"I've never seen anything like it," Sammy said, shaking his head. "The kid's just a wing-eating *machine*."

"Do you even, like, *taste* anything before it slides down your throat?" Gabe asked.

Mickey stopped chewing long enough to grunt.

"I think that means yes," Gabe said. He looked at Mickey again. "Nod if that meant yes."

Mickey nodded happily and burped.

Katelyn shook her head in dismay as she watched him.

"I want you to know something," she said. "And I mean this from the bottom of my heart, okay? You are one disgusting human being."

Mickey smiled broadly, his greasy lips shining.

Katelyn sighed and looked at the others. "I don't know why I bother. The boy has no shame. You call him disgusting and he practically wants to hug you. Which"—she glared at Mickey—"you can forget about doing, nerd. Unless you want a kick in the you-know-whats."

"Ooooh!" the other Orioles murmured. "In the you-know-whats!"

Mickey smiled again and flashed Katelyn the peace sign with two orange-stained fingers.

"Wonder what the world record is for eating wings?" Sammy said as Mickey continued to chew.

Hunter piped up. "I got that. It's three hundred and sixty-three wings in a half hour."

The others turned to stare at him.

"What?" he said. "I looked it up when I knew we were coming here. A woman, Molly Schuyler. She ate three hundred and sixty-three wings at Wing Bowl Twenty-two. She weighs only one hundred and twenty-five pounds, I think. But don't quote me."

"Thank you, Mr. Wikipedia," Sammy said. "That was very enlightening."

"You're welcome," Hunter said.

Gabe nodded in Mickey's direction. "Give this guy a few years and he'll challenge that lady. You watch. My man M-Dog's a beast!"

"Okay, enough about the stupid wings," Sammy said, looking at Mickey. "What we want to know is: are you gonna kick Zoom's butt or what?"

Mickey considered the question for a moment and shrugged. He sucked the meat off another wing and tossed it on the small mountain of bones, then took a big gulp from a water glass.

"Thing is, Zoom's right," he said finally. "I *should* eat more salad. I was mad the other day, when he first said it, sure. But the kid had a point. Just look at me."

He patted his ample belly and sighed contentedly. "But if all I ate was salad, I'd miss all this fun at Augie's. Besides, Katelyn says she likes me just the way I am. She says I'm *hot*."

"Oh, puh-leeze!" Katelyn said, turning red. "You could only *wish*, nerd."

"There's no use denying it, Katelyn," Mickey said, deadpan. "It's written all over your face each time you look at me. You think I'm *smokin'*. Might as well admit it."

At this, Katelyn lunged across the table, nearly knocking over their drinks, and got right in Mickey's face.

"ZIP IT, NERD!" she roared. "NOW YOU'RE BEING TOTALLY DELUSIONAL!"

Mickey grinned as the rest of the Orioles cracked up. But he quickly grew pensive again—well, as pensive as a kid could be with gobs of orange sauce smeared all over his shirt.

Earlier that day he had told a few of the Orioles about Zoom's salad-line put-down after the Red Sox game. Soon Mickey regretted opening his mouth, because his friends had spent the rest of practice shooting dirty looks at their new pitcher, who seemed puzzled by this treatment.

Sure, Zoom's a ginormous jerk, Mickey thought. But this is between him and me. It's not fair for me to drag my friends into it. If it'll help Zoom's pitching and get us a shot at the Huntington team, I can take a few more zingers about the size of my gut.

On the other hand, Mickey no longer had to wonder if he was the only Oriole who couldn't stand Zoom. No, it was clear from the way his friends were talking that they felt the same way about the new kid.

That wasn't good—having players take sides and turn on a teammate. That could break any team apart—even one as close as the Orioles.

"So let me get this straight," Sammy was saying now, a note of exasperation in his voice. "You're just going to let Zoom get away with it? Dissing you like that? Practically calling you a porker? And in front of what's-her-name?"

"Abby," Mickey said.

"Whatever," Sammy said. "That's just not right."

After mentioning Abby's name, Mickey suppressed a smile. The two had continued to talk for another fifteen minutes after Zoom and his boys left the snowball stand the other night. Mickey had to admit he was beginning to like her more and more.

Mickey still didn't know—and couldn't guess—what Zoom had said that had made her laugh so hysterically. Zoom didn't seem like a funny guy, since he was stone-faced whenever he was around the Orioles.

It didn't matter now, though, because Abby's delight had been replaced by outrage at Zoom's dig. Over and over again she had told Mickey to "just ignore the big idiot." And she had talked earnestly about how mean kids could be to one another, especially on social media, where anyone could post something nasty and remain anonymous.

"If someone ever wrote something on Facebook about me being ugly, I think I'd just *die*," Abby had said at one point.

Yeah, Mickey had thought, looking into those dark eyes. Like that would ever happen.

The other thing Mickey liked about Abby was that she seemed to know more about baseball than most guys her age—and maybe even more than Katelyn, who was a walking encyclopedia about the game.

Not that he planned to spend a lot of time talking about, say, the nuances of the hit-and-run play with Abby. But it was kind of cool to think that she might appreciate it if he did.

"You have to teach Zoom a lesson. Period," Sammy was saying now. "Otherwise, he'll just keep doggin' you."

"Yeah," Hunter said. "Look, you're bigger than him . . ."

"And stronger than him . . ." Gabe said.

"And definitely dumber than him," Katelyn said. "Way, *way* dumber. If he hits you in the head, it'll feel like cotton, since there's nothing up there."

She flashed an angelic smile and went back to eating her wings.

Mickey grinned. He turned to the others and nodded in Katelyn's direction.

"Don't let her fool you," he said. "She's crazy about me. Just has a funny way of showing it sometimes."

Katelyn picked up a bone and fired it at his head. He ducked and the bone hit the wall behind him.

"Security!" he cried, standing and waving his hands. "Disturbance at table fifteen! This young lady needs to be escorted from the premises, please!"

Everyone laughed. But a moment later, Mickey grew serious.

"Let's not talk about Zoom anymore," he said, pushing the plate of wings away. "It's killing my appetite."

The truth was, Mickey wasn't sure what to do about Zoom right now.

Confront him and demand an apology? Pretend the whole thing never happened?

Maybe, he thought, Zoom was actually feeling sorry for what he'd said the other day at the snowball stand.

Maybe he regretted that ridiculous grandstanding strategy of intentionally walking a Red Sox batter just to show off his pickoff move—which could have been disastrous for the Orioles if it had led to a loss.

Maybe one day he'd see the light—the term Mickey's dad always used—and stop being such a jerk.

Yeah, right.

Well, Mickey thought, a guy can dream.

He sighed and looked at the uneaten wings, only now they were making his stomach queasy.

Why did it feel like his problems with Zoom were just beginning?

Mickey was sitting at the kitchen table the next morning when his dad appeared in the doorway, whistling cheerfully.

"Take a ride with me," he said, scooping his car keys off the counter. "And bring your gear."

"My gear? Where are we going?" Mickey asked.

But his dad just shook his head.

"No time for yakking," he said. "We're late as it is."

They drove to the outskirts of town, past the rolling green hills behind York Middle School and Eddie Murray Field and past Smith Clove Park, where the Orioles occasionally worked out when the other fields were flooded.

Okay, Mickey thought, so we're not headed to some impromptu practice to keep us sharp for a late-season push. Unless we're practicing on the side of a road somewhere. Or in a cornfield. Which would make it kind of tough to see the ball.

After fifteen minutes, they pulled up to a low-slung green building with well-manicured shrubs and flower beds out front and a parking lot on the side.

Mickey stared out the window. Something about the place looked familiar. He had seen it before—he was positive. Maybe it was in a TV commercial, or on the cover of a sports magazine, or a brochure or . . .

Then it hit him.

"NO-O-O!" he yelled, wide-eyed. "Is this . . . ?"

He turned back to see his dad smiling and nodding.

"No *way*!" Mickey shouted. He leaped from the car and sprinted to the front of the building. There it was, the big sign with the logo of a catcher coming out of his crouch to gun down another would-be base stealer, the sign that read:

RON DILLMAN'S CATCHING CLINICS—
LEARN FROM THE BEST TO BE THE BEST

Ron Dillman! Mickey could hardly believe it. Dillman was generally regarded as the greatest catcher in Orioles history, even though Mickey was convinced Matt Wieters would one day hold that honor. Now retired, Dillman ran a series of popular catching clinics and was considered one of the finest teachers of young catchers on the East Coast.

Mickey yelped excitedly and hugged his dad as they walked inside.

"Thank you, thank you, thank you! But how did you . . . why did you . . . ?" Mickey blurted, his thoughts racing. "I know these sessions aren't cheap, and there's probably a waiting list, and—"

His dad patted his arm. "Don't worry about that. I know you're having a hard time with a certain new pitcher of ours—although I'm not exactly sure why, since he's been lights-out for us. And we're closing in on the championship, aren't we? But this is just a little thank-you for hanging in there. Just go have fun today, okay? And learn something."

Ron Dillman had a craggy, sunburned face and a bushy brown mustache and, at six-foot-two, was built along the lines of a stand-up freezer. His thick fingers were swollen and gnarled after a fifteen-year career in the big leagues.

There were four other boys in the session and Dillman began with a rousing pep talk that got everyone majorly pumped.

"Let's start with the obvious: you boys are a darn special bunch," Dillman announced in a booming voice. "You play the most demanding position in baseball. And the toughest. Don't ever let anyone tell you differently. You're like the Army Rangers or the Navy SEALs of the game.

"Think about all you do during the course of a game," he continued. "You're involved in every pitch. You have to block balls in the dirt, leap for balls over your head, lunge for the ones outside. You have to keep track of the count on hitters. You have to throw out base stealers. You have to cover bunts with a catlike quickness."

Now a sly smile lit up his face.

"Some of you call pitches during games and a lot of you don't anymore. But whether you call pitches or not, you have to *deal* with pitchers. And that's no day at the beach, right? Trust me when I tell you this: all pitchers, to one degree or another, are head cases. Total and absolute head cases. And prima donnas, too. You can take that to the bank."

The boys looked at one another and chuckled.

Gee, Mickey thought, I know someone who fits that description.

"And we haven't even gotten to the hard part of catching yet!" Dillman went on, his voice rising. "You have to wear a ton of bulky equipment that restricts your mobility, limits your peripheral vision, and makes a ninety-degree day feel like a sauna in hell! How's that for a nice thank-you for playing the game's most important position?"

Now there were knowing nods all around.

"And that's *still* not the hardest part!" Dillman said, dropping his voice dramatically. "No, we haven't talked yet about what it's like to get whacked with a bat on the shoulder or elbow or wrist from a hitter's backswing. We haven't talked about what it's like to be in a bone-jarring collision with a base runner at the plate—although, yes, they're trying to outlaw that and make the game as namby-pamby as, I don't know, croquet.

"And let us not forget, gentlemen," he continued in a near whisper, "we haven't talked about what it feels like when a ball bounces in the dirt and catches you right below the cup, in that, um, critical area of barely any protection, where you experience the most excruciating pain of all. Am I right?"

Five boys winced and nodded while instinctively drawing their knees together.

With that, Dillman smiled beatifically and spread his arms wide.

"And yet, despite all the pain and sweat and hardship, you *still* love catching!" he concluded. "That, my young friends, is what makes you so special! And I'm darned proud and honored to welcome you to our little clinic. Now let's get to work! By the time you leave here, you will all be the best young catchers you can be! I guaran-freaking-tee it!"

Now the boys were on their feet, whooping and high-fiving. For the next two hours, Dillman and his aides ran them through a series of drills that covered every aspect of playing the position.

They worked on the basic setup for a catcher: feet positioned shoulder width apart, weight evenly distrib-uted, glove hand extended to give the pitcher a nice target, throwing hand behind the body to protect it from foul balls.

They worked on catching the ball with runners on base, moving the glove-side leg forward, rotating the shoulders, bringing the glove and ball up to the ear while readying the throwing hand for the transfer in case of a steal attempt.

They worked on when to whip off the catcher's mask (pop flies, chasing wild pitches and passed balls) and when to leave it on (steals, plays at the plate, bunts).

"And, boys, you probably don't have to worry about this right now. But never, *ever* take that mask off if your team gets in a brawl with the other team!" Dillman bellowed. "I mean, how dumb would that be? You're the only player on the field wearing any kind of protection and you *take it off* when punches start flying?"

He looked incredulously from one boy to another.

"Any catcher who takes his mask off in the middle of a donnybrook—you can look that word up when you get home—is nothing but a fool!" he roared.

The two hours seemed to go by quickly. Mickey was

like a sponge sopping up all this information, even though he was already familiar with much of it, having studied the position since he was a little kid.

It was after a final drill on how to field bunts—with the bare hand if the ball has stopped, Dillman said, with the glove if it's still rolling—that Mickey became aware of a conversation between two dads in the waiting area behind them.

Mickey didn't mean to eavesdrop. But one man's voice in particular was loud enough to be heard in Oregon.

". . . pitched against my son's team last year," the man was saying now. "Oh, you should have seen this kid! Ton of talent, but a royal pain in the butt. Tried to stare down each batter. Thought he was better than everyone else. Barked at his dad, barked at his teammates. A kid with the proverbial million-dollar arm and ten-cent brain—that's what he was."

The man shook his head in disgust.

"Anyway, we don't have to face him again," he continued. "The family moved out of the neighborhood when the season was over. Don't know where they went. But, good riddance. Bet there wasn't much of a going-away party."

Mickey's heart was hammering in his chest. He gathered up his gear and walked over to where the man was standing and tried to keep his voice casual.

"Excuse me," he said. "That boy you were talking about? With the great arm? And the, um, not-so-great brain? What was his name?"

The man furrowed his brow and didn't answer right away.

"Don't remember his last name," he said finally. "Come to think of it, I don't even know his first name. All I remember is, he had some goofy nickname."

Mickey groaned inwardly.

"Zip or Zoom, I think it was," the old man added. "Zoom, that was it. Some piece of work, that kid."

Mickey managed to stammer, "Th-thanks." He waved to Dillman and his aides and headed out into the bright sunshine. His dad was leaning against their car, reading a newspaper. He looked up and smiled as Mickey approached.

"So?" his dad said. "Have fun? Learn anything new?"

"Oh, yeah," Mickey said, jumping in the front seat. "Learned a lot, actually."

He had definitely learned something new about Zoom, all right. But there was no point in passing along that little tidbit to his dad, who wouldn't believe him anyway. And probably wouldn't care, either.

No, why would he? Zoom was pitching lights-out! And the Orioles were closing in on the championship!

Nothing else really seemed to matter right now.

The doorbell rang at nine a.m., followed by the kind of urgent knocking someone might use to alert someone that his house was on fire.

It *has* to be her, Mickey thought.

He answered the door and groaned inwardly. Yes, there she was: Katelyn. In one hand she held what appeared to be a thick sheet of cream-colored paper.

"What's up, nerd?" she said. "Wanna read something that'll totally make you puke?"

Mickey considered how to answer.

"Sure," he said finally. "Like most people, that's my favorite thing to do. Especially first thing in the morning."

"Don't start with the sarcasm," Katelyn said, brushing past him. "You're not good at it. Not good at a lot of other things, too. But we won't get into that now."

Mickey shook his head and watched her stroll into the family room and plop down on a couch.

Long ago, he had decided that living around the corner from Katelyn had both advantages and disadvantages.

The good thing was that there was always someone

nearby to play catch with, or shoot baskets with, or toss around a football with.

The bad thing was that you got called "nerd" a lot. Plus she could show up at your door at all hours with weird requests and off-the-wall questions, like today's stunner.

"Know what this is?" she said, tossing the paper on the counter.

"Another love letter to me?" Mickey said, grinning. "Katelyn, this is really getting embarrassing. People are starting to talk."

She shot him a look.

"Don't start," she said. "This, for your information, is the Huntington Yankees' newsletter."

"They have their own *newsletter*?" Mickey asked.

"Apparently," Katelyn said. "My mom works in Huntington. She picked this up in a drugstore."

The newsletter had a slick, professional look to it. The lead story at the top of the page was headlined in big, block letters: A TEAM FOR THE AGES. It was accompanied by an oversize photo of a smiling Al "Money" Mayhew, leaning on a bat while watching the Yankees practice in the background, looking like a proud general surveying his troops on the eve of a battle.

Mickey began to read aloud:

" 'There's a reason Al Mayhew, one of the most respected youth baseball coaches in the country, has earned the nickname "Money." In his eleven years at the helm of the Huntington Yankees, he's guided the team to nine league titles and countless tournament wins and postseason honors. Al's encyclopedic knowledge of the game, his strong work ethic, and ability to get the best out of his young charges have again propelled the Yankees to one of the best records in the team's storied history.'"

Katelyn snickered. "Yeah, right. Nothing about him illegally recruiting players from all over. Or holding mandatory four-hour practices. Or stealing the other teams' signs. Nothing about him making sure it's his buddies who umpire his team's games."

"No," Mickey said, "none of that's in here. Absolutely shocking, isn't it?"

He continued reading:

"'But as is typical with the ever-modest Coach Mayhew, he deflects praise for his efforts and credits the team's success to the outstanding players he'd had over the years. "I always tell my boys to play clean, follow the rules, and have respect for your opponent. To paraphrase what a great man said many years ago: It's not about whether you win or lose, it's about how you play the game."'"

"AAARGGHH! That did it!" Katelyn said, sticking a finger down her throat. "I'm officially gonna spew!"

Without looking up, Mickey pointed down the hall. "You know where the bathroom is," he said.

He went back to the article:

"'This year's team is once again loaded with talent and should have no problem posting yet another undefeated season. Led by Al's son, all-star catcher Marvin "Moose" Mayhew, the Yankees—'"

"*Marvin?*" Katelyn interrupted. "His real name's *Marvin*? No wonder he goes by Moose."

"'—feature a power-laden offense, airtight defense, and

sensational pitching,'" Mickey continued reading. "'Like so many of its famous predecessors, it's a Yankees team that appears to have absolutely no weaknesses.'"

Katelyn rolled her eyes. "Translation: 'We're the greatest team ever assembled and nobody can beat us, so don't even try.' Ooooh, that makes me so mad I could scream! Please, don't read any more. It makes me want to just . . . *strangle* someone."

"As long as it's not me," Mickey said. He scanned the rest of the page and whistled softly.

"Look at this!" he said. "A photo of each player, along with a miniprofile."

"Like they're rock stars or something!" Katelyn said. "Can you believe it? God, I would *love* to play those arrogant dorks and beat their butts!"

"Me, too," Mickey said. "Okay, let's just read what they say about your boy Moose Mayhew."

"*Marvin,*" Katelyn corrected. "If we're going to talk about budding legends, at least use the kid's real name."

"Fine," Mickey said. He went back to reading:

"'The Yankees' cleanup hitter and one of the most feared sluggers in the league, Moose'—er, *Marvin*—'Mayhew is once again the cornerstone of the vaunted Yankees offense. But his rocket arm and outstanding defensive abilities behind the plate have also played a key part in the team's success this season. While being interviewed for this article, he asked that we give a shout-out to his new girlfriend, Katelyn Morris—'"

"*WHAT?!*" Katelyn cried.

"Just messing with you," Mickey said, chuckling. He

threw up his hands and ducked. "Please, no freak-outs, no punches, no strangulations. Be cool."

Katelyn glared at him. "Nerd, you are *so* asking for it," she said. But Mickey was relieved to see her smile seconds later.

She snatched the newsletter and crumpled it into a ball.

"Okay, that's enough of that," she said. "Do you know I've actually *dreamed* about what it would be like to beat them and their slimeball coach?"

Mickey pretended to dab tears from his eyes. "That hurts, Katelyn. *Really* hurts. Here I thought you only dreamed about me."

Katelyn shook her head. "You're really pushing it, nerd. Do you have a death wish? Is that it?"

"Okay, okay," Mickey said, laughing and holding up his hands. "But the fact is, you *could* end up playing the Yankees. It's not like a total fantasy. We're having a pretty good season, aren't we? And even though Zoom's a major pain in the butt, he could be just what we need to win the whole league. So don't give up hope, girl."

Katelyn nodded. Now there was a mischievous glint in her eyes.

"If we ever *did* play them," she said, "think your dad would let us chant 'MARV-IN! MAR-VIN!' when that big dork Moose is up?"

"Uh, I'd say that's a definite no," Mickey said.

"Too bad," she said. "Another great fantasy bites the dust."

Mickey found it hard to concentrate. The Orioles were loosening up before their big game against the Rays, needing two more wins to catch the front-running Indians, who had lost their last game and seemed ripe to be overtaken.

But all he could think was: Why did I open my big mouth—*again*?

Because right now his teammates were killing him.

"Oooooh, did I hear someone's just back from the Ron Dillman clinic?" Katelyn said loudly as she threw with Sammy on the sidelines. "That's the premier catchers' clinic around, isn't it?"

"Yeah, you gotta be an off-the-charts prospect to attend," Sammy said. "Or else your daddy has to plunk down a nice chunk of cash to get you in."

"*Everybody's* heard of the Ron Dillman clinic," Corey chimed in.

"Absolutely everybody," Evan said. "They've heard of it in China, India, Africa—all over the world!"

Mickey knew his face was turning red. But there was no

way to stop the teasing. He had screwed up, pure and simple, telling Hunter about this great clinic he'd been lucky enough to attend over the weekend.

Hunter had waited, oh, maybe five seconds before spreading this information to the rest of the team.

That's all it took for the rag-fest to begin.

Now it was in full swing.

There was nothing to do but wait for the jokes to die down. It was death by a thousand paper cuts, sure. But at this point, what could you do?

"When we go to Augie's for Wing Night, are you going to require your own private booth?" Katelyn asked. "Because you're such a big Dillman superstar alum and all?"

"Yeah," Sammy said. "And you'll have some big bouncer dude working the velvet rope to keep all us little people away, right?"

"Even better," Hunter said, "Mickey and Zoom could share a booth in a specially cordoned-off section. It would be like the Elite Arms/Ron Dillman booth! And they could sign autographs and look down on the rest of us while they sit up there wolfing down their wings. Which, of course, would be on the house."

"Of *course*," Katelyn said. She yelled to Mickey, "Nerd, you should call your agent and tell him to get the ball rolling on that right away."

The Orioles laughed so hard that even Mickey had to join in.

"Remind me to never tell you another thing as long as I live," he said to Hunter, who shrugged sheepishly, as if to say, *Come on, bro, what did you expect?*

"Speaking of our star pitcher, what time do we think the Z-Train will roll in this afternoon?" Gabe asked, scanning the parking lot.

"Oh, please!" Katelyn said. "It's only half an hour before game time. You can't expect the boy to get here in time to stretch and take batting practice, can you?" She shot a look at Mickey. "Our coach has apparently decided that certain big-shot pitchers can show up whenever they want."

Mickey felt his cheeks get warm again. Over the years he'd heard from other kids who played for their dads that it could sometimes suck being the coach's son. This was definitely one of those times.

Mickey wanted desperately to stick up for his dad. But he was just as ticked off as the other kids about Zoom getting free license. No, check that. Mickey was even *more* ticked off than the rest of the team, since Zoom was insisting on calling pitches.

In fact, it was another fifteen minutes before Zoom and his gloomy-looking posse arrived. As he walked down the left-field line with Mickey to warm up, Zoom draped an arm around his catcher.

"Feeling good about this game, big man," Zoom said. "In fact, I got a plan."

Mickey braced himself.

Zoom's last plan—the let's-walk-'em-and-pick-'em-off plan—hadn't worked out so well.

"I can't wait to hear it," Mickey said drily.

But Zoom shook his head.

"No, better not tell you right now," Zoom said. "It's top secret."

Mickey recoiled. *Top secret?* Nuclear missile codes were top secret. The new iPad software to be unveiled next week was top secret.

But a plan for a baseball game? Weren't they on the same team?

Zoom clapped him on the back. "You'll see what we're doing as soon as the game starts. It's killer, too."

Unfortunately, as soon as the first Rays batter dug in, Zoom's plan became painfully obvious: he had decided not to throw any fastballs. Instead, from the very first pitch, he began relying solely on his curve and changeup.

This meant that the Orioles and Rays—and everyone else in the stands—were treated to the weird sight of Zoom sticking out his tongue or closing his eyes before each pitch to signal his catcher as to what was coming.

"What a clown act," Mickey muttered to himself after the first Rays batter walked on a 3–2 breaking ball a mile outside.

It didn't take long for Zoom's facial gyrations to provoke a cascade of snickers and jeers from the Rays dugout.

"Whoa! Pitcher's spazzing out!" a voice cried.

"Hey, what're you doing with that tongue, Pitch?" bellowed another voice. "And those eyes! Those are some *seriously* ugly looks you're throwing!"

It didn't help that Zoom was struggling with his control. And without throwing his blazing fastball at all, he was fooling no one when he put the ball over the plate.

After the next batter walked, only a nice 6-4-3 double play started by Sammy on a two-hopper up the middle prevented the Rays from scoring. And only a running catch by Katelyn on a long fly ball to right got the Orioles out of the inning without giving up a run.

"What's he *doing*?" Gabe hissed, staring at Zoom as the pitcher plopped down at the end of the bench, his usual spot.

"I don't know," Mickey said, shaking his head. "He's like the weather around here: something new every five minutes."

The Orioles took a 2–0 lead on a one-run single by Sammy, and Mickey's double into the left-center gap off the Rays starter, Josh Grogan, one of the better pitchers in the league. But Zoom continued with his tongue wagging and eye closing and no-fastballs policy when he took the mound again, and he gave up a single and a walk.

Between pitches, Mickey kept glancing at the dugout, wondering if his dad had seen enough and was ready to give Zoom the hook. But the coach stood impassively on the top step, arms folded across his chest, studying the pitcher as if trying to figure out what in God's name had gotten into him.

Zoom managed to get the next Rays batter on a pop foul to Ethan behind first, and the next kid was called out when he tried to bunt and ran into the ball on his way to first. But another single put the Rays at 2–1 before Zoom got the final out on a slow roller to the mound.

It wasn't until the third inning, as they took the field, that Zoom said to his catcher, "Going back to the heat now, big man. Just so you know."

Gee, thanks for sharing, Mickey thought.

And that's *not* top secret?

On the other hand, Mickey was greatly relieved that Zoom had come to his senses. Maybe, he thought, all the weirdness is over.

But it wasn't.

In fact, things quickly got even weirder after Zoom blew three fastballs past the Rays lead-off hitter.

When the last pitch popped into Mickey's glove and the ump bellowed, "Stee-rike three!," Zoom pretended to pull a sword from his belt and make a slashing motion.

At first Mickey didn't get it.

Then it dawned on him: Zoom was slashing a big Z in the air!

And the Z wasn't for "Zorro," either.

Mickey was so stunned he forgot to whip the ball down to third.

In the next instant, his dad popped out of the dugout, called time, and made a beeline for the mound with a grim expression. He signaled Mickey to join him.

This could be interesting, Mickey thought.

He hadn't seen that look in his dad's eyes in a long time.

Mickey's dad got right in Zoom's face.

"That thing you just did?" his dad said. "With your hand?"

"What thing?" Zoom asked innocently.

"That . . . *thing*," Coach said. "After the strikeout?"

He jabbed his hand awkwardly in the air. It was a totally lame imitation of Zoom's slash move, Mickey thought. But it got the point across.

"Don't . . . *ever* . . . do . . . that . . . again," his dad hissed.

"*Ever?*" Zoom said.

"Right," Mickey's dad said. "Ever. We don't do that on this team. We don't show up our opponents. Ever."

Zoom looked quizzically at Mickey, then back to his coach.

"But that's my new signature move!" Zoom protested. "It gets me pumped! You know, after a strikeout! Gets the adrenaline going, gets the crowd into it, gets my team-mates jacked, gets—"

"Lose it," Mickey's dad growled. The tip of his nose was

now about three inches from Zoom's nose. "This isn't up for debate. Do I make myself clear?"

Yay, Dad, Mickey thought. Way to take control. Way to come down hard—even if it did take you a few weeks.

Zoom's eyes were blazing. He stared at Coach, neither one of them blinking for several seconds.

Finally, Zoom looked away. He bent down and picked up the rosin bag. He squeezed it tightly and gazed at it as if lost in thought.

"Fine," he said sullenly, tossing the bag down.

Without another word, Mickey's dad turned and headed back to the dugout.

Mickey looked at Zoom and shrugged.

"Meeting adjourned, I guess," he said.

Even though he was thrilled that his dad had finally put the big jerk in his place, Mickey wanted to say something else to Zoom.

He wasn't sure what. But he wanted to say something encouraging, something to remind the pitcher to keep his focus, to command his fastball, to just win, baby, to keep the O's on track for a trophy no matter how pissed he was.

But the look on Zoom's face made it clear he was in no mood for conversation.

Zoom stalked around the mound for a moment, trying to compose himself. The Orioles could tell he was furious. So could the next batter for the Rays, who dug in nervously, then quickly stepped out, took a deep breath, and dug in again.

Zoom was throwing harder than ever before, the ball

almost whistling through the air before it smacked into Mickey's glove.

He struck the kid out on four pitches. He threw so hard that the third pitch flew over the batter's head and crashed into the backstop with a loud *THWAP!* But he came back with a fastball on the inside of the plate that totally hand-cuffed the boy, who seemed relieved to trudge back to the dugout.

This time there was no theatrical *Z* slash after the strikeout. Instead, as the Orioles whipped the ball around the infield, Zoom made a point of staring in at his coach.

Ooooh, big mistake doing that, Mickey thought. Dad doesn't go for that stuff at all.

But the Orioles had never seen Zoom throw the way he was throwing now. This isn't even fair, Mickey thought. The Rays will be lucky to foul a pitch off, never mind get a base hit.

Zoom struck out the next batter, too, on three straight fastballs. The last one cut the heart of the plate, the kid swinging so late and looking so foolish that Mickey almost felt sorry for him.

As Zoom walked slowly off the mound, he glared at the Rays as they took the field.

On his jog back to the dugout, Mickey saw his dad shaking his head.

When everyone was on the bench, Coach said in a loud voice, "Danny, warm up. You're pitching next inning."

The rest of the Orioles stole glances at Zoom. Coach had delivered a message, all right. The message they'd all been waiting for. Danny was coming in earlier than usual because of Zoom's classless showing off.

The coach who had fallen in love with Zoom's arm and put up with all his crap from the very beginning had apparently had enough.

But it was tough to read Zoom's reaction. He plopped down at the end of the bench again and sat hunched over with a towel draped around his head.

The Orioles failed to score in their half of the inning. It was clear that Josh Grogan had settled into a groove now, deftly mixing his fastball and changeup to keep the Orioles hitters off balance.

After taking the field in the top of the fourth, all the Orioles fielders gathered on the mound to give Danny a pep talk.

"Don't be nervous, nerd," Katelyn said.

"I'm not," Danny said.

"And don't worry about the fact that we're clinging to a one-run lead with the season on the line," Sammy said.

"Is this supposed to calm me down?" Danny asked.

"And don't think about how when the Rays pull Josh, they'll probably bring in Bobby Oneida, who we don't hit at all," Hunter said. "Meaning we kind of seriously need you to shut these guys down, dude."

Danny shook his head in amazement. "And this is where you tell me there's no pressure, right?"

"Right," Evan said. "It's just another game."

Mickey couldn't believe what he was hearing.

"That did it—get out of here!" he said, taking charge and shooing the others away.

Mickey felt bad. He had screwed up by letting too many of the O's talk to Danny. It went against his firm belief that the only two people who should ever talk to the pitcher during a game were the coach and the catcher. Otherwise, a pitcher could get overwhelmed, bombarded with too many voices giving him a different version of what Mickey called the you-da-man-but-don't-blow-it speech.

What was it that his dad called it when too many kids were jabbering at the pitcher? Psychobabble? Mickey wasn't exactly sure what that meant. But it sounded right—at least the *babble* part.

He took the ball, placed it firmly in Danny's glove, and said, "Don't think. Just throw."

That, Mickey thought, should be the mantra of every pitcher at this level. In fact, it should be written on T-shirts and handed out to them at the beginning of the season. And each pitcher should be required to wear it under his jersey on game day, as a reminder.

Danny, though, was already thinking too much.

He got into trouble immediately. Instead of challenging the hitters with his fastball, he tried hitting the corners of the plate and missed miserably.

The result was a walk to the first two batters and an accompanying sigh of frustration from the Orioles fielders. Then Danny got lucky when the next kid swung at a pitch in the dirt for strike three. But another walk loaded the bases. And when Danny finally decided to go directly at the hitters instead of trying to fool them, he threw a fat pitch over the plate that the Rays catcher promptly drilled to right field for a two-run single.

Just like that it was Rays 3, Orioles 2.

As he watched the meltdown, Mickey thought: Going from Zoom on the mound to Danny—especially when he's this shaky—is like going from Yale to kindergarten. It was fun to catch Danny, since Mickey could call pitches and flash signs again. But when the pitcher was afraid to give the other team something to hit, it made for long, hot, discouraging innings.

Danny bore down and got the next two batters on a weak comebacker to the mound and a pop foul to Hunter. But the minute he walked dejectedly off the mound, Katelyn was in his ear.

"Seriously, nerd?" Katelyn said. "You're going to start walking people now?"

"It wasn't exactly my game plan," Danny said, throwing his glove on the bench. "I didn't go out there thinking, 'Hey, let's walk a few guys! That might be fun!'"

He watched Katelyn scowl and ball her fist. "And don't punch me in the shoulder, either," Danny said, flinching reflexively. "I gotta pitch."

"Someone should punch you in the brain," Katelyn muttered, stomping away.

But the Orioles rallied in the fifth. Whatever magic their old nemesis, Bobby Oneida, had once had was now gone as they took a 4–3 lead on back-to-back doubles by Corey and Spencer and Ethan's single. And Danny stopped nibbling at the Rays batters when he took the mound in the sixth.

Danny's fastball would never be intimidating, Mickey thought. But when he threw it for strikes and trusted his defense to make plays, the kid could be an effective reliever.

And he was more than effective here in the sixth, getting the first two Rays batters on infield grounders and striking out the third batter to close out the win.

After the final out, Mickey punched a fist in the air and jogged out to high-five his pitcher. Just then they heard a loud war whoop coming from right field.

Looking up, they saw Katelyn sprinting toward them, a huge grin on her face, her arms opened wide.

"Talk about mood swings," Danny murmured before Katelyn wrapped him in a bear hug and the other Orioles descended on them, laughing and clapping them on the back.

Mickey stepped back and watched the celebration. He looked at his dad, who smiled and gave him the thumbs-up sign.

Everyone knew this was a huge win. One more and another Indians loss meant they'd be tied for first place, another step closer to the championship and their goal of a shot at the mighty Huntington Yankees.

And if Zoom could get his head on straight and keep throwing as hard as he did in the third inning—when every pitch had rocked Mickey's glove and felt like it cracked eighty on the radar gun—well, maybe the Orioles could even . . .

Suddenly a thought jolted him.

Where was Zoom? He wasn't jumping up and down with the others on the field. A glance at the dugout showed he wasn't there, either.

Mickey looked out at the parking lot. There, in the gathering dusk, he saw a black SUV pull up. A kid wearing an

Orioles jersey, his head hanging down, trudged toward it. Trailing behind him were three other forlorn-looking figures.

"Guess he wanted to beat the traffic," a familiar voice said.

Mickey turned and saw Gabe staring out at the parking lot, too.

"The boy definitely has some issues," Gabe said, shaking his head. "But we kinda need him now, don't we?"

Mickey didn't have a cell phone. This was an eternal source of irritation to him. Even though he was almost thirteen, his parents had made it clear: there would be no cell phone in his immediate future. And there was no sense whining about it.

Mickey knew his mom and dad were afraid he'd waste time endlessly texting his friends and playing stupid mobile games and watching dumb YouTube clips of kids parachuting off roofs with bedsheets, or dogs wearing swim goggles while surfing in Maui.

All of which sounded great to Mickey.

But his parents wouldn't relent.

"You'd have your head buried in that phone twenty-four-seven," his dad had said. "Uh uh. Not gonna happen."

"What am I, an Amish kid?" Mickey grumbled. "You're banning technology from my life?"

"Call the abuse hotline," his mom, Karen, said with a grin. "Tell them you have the meanest mom and dad in the whole world."

The only good thing about not having a cell phone,

Mickey thought, was that it meant he would never *lose* a cell phone. Which meant he'd never have to spend the whole day quaking in terror at the prospect of reporting a lost phone to his parents, the way so many of his friends seemed to do.

So when the phone in the kitchen rang early the next morning, Mickey knew there was a good chance it was for him. How else could his buds reach him, given that his parents insisted on forcing their kid to live in the cellular Dark Ages?

He looked at the caller ID and saw: ELLIOTT, ABIGAIL.

He felt his heart pounding as he picked up.

"What are you doing, star?" said the voice on the other end.

Mickey smiled. No "hi" to start the conversation. No "Hey, how are you?" That was Abby, as he was finding out. The girl got right down to business, just like on the first night he had met her: *Hey, you! Buy my snowballs or else!*

But how to answer her question?

Should he tell her the truth about what he was doing now? Sitting at the table in his pajamas, eating a bowl of Cap'n Crunch?

Which, Mickey thought, was probably worse for a kid's well-being than any cell phone.

"Oh," he said finally, "I'm studying algebra and science, then finishing up a major book report. Y'know, kind of like I do every Saturday morning."

Abby snorted. "Right, like I believe any of that. Why don't you come down to the field? The little kids are playing, and business is awful. They don't have any money and their parents are cheapos. Which means I'm super bored."

YESSS! Mickey thought, pumping his fist. But he tried to keep his voice calm.

"Okay," he said. "I'll put these textbooks away and be right down."

"You crack me up, star," Abby said with a chuckle. "You really do." Then she hung up.

Ten minutes later, Mickey jumped on his bike and headed for Eddie Murray Field. It was another hot summer day, with a hint of rain in the air. But the field was less than a mile away if you cut through two neighborhoods and around the shopping center.

As he pedaled along, Mickey wondered: Is that why Abby called me? 'Cause I live so close to the field? And I can get down there fast when she's bored?

Or did she call because I—how did she put it—crack her up with my biting wit? Or because she's never seen such a handsome specimen in her entire life?

Quickly he decided he didn't really care *why* she had called. He was just thrilled that she did.

When he got to the snowball stand, Abby was perched on a stool behind the counter. She was holding a rolled-up piece of cardboard in one hand and looking nervously from side to side.

"Expecting trouble?" Mickey asked. "I don't know how much good that, uh, weapon of yours will do. I don't see the bad guys saying, 'Uh-oh, better leave her alone—she's packing *cardboard*!'"

Abby made a face.

"Very funny," she said. "But you know *exactly* why I have this."

"Um, actually, I don't," Mickey said.

Abby looked around again and dropped her voice dramatically.

"Bees," she said. "They're coming. Oh, yes, any day now. I can feel it. The owner said to be on the lookout. And the girl working yesterday thought she might have seen one."

"*Might* have seen one," Mickey repeated.

"That's good enough for me," Abby said. "We're on high alert here."

She came out from behind the counter and led Mickey over to one of the picnic tables. Not far away, two teams in the under-ten division were playing, their voices echoing off the tall trees that ringed the outfield.

Abby sat down heavily and frowned.

"Star," she said, "I told a fib. I didn't ask you to come down just because I was bored. I need some advice, too. And you're the perfect person to talk to."

Me? Mickey thought. She's asking *me* for advice? About what? Which kind of Cap'n Crunch I'd recommend? Peanut Butter Crunch versus All Berries?

"I told you I play softball," Abby continued. "Anyway, the coach of our team is leaving. He's taking a job in California. And my dad has been asked to replace him. He said he won't do it if I don't want him to. And I don't know how I feel about it."

Her eyes seemed to bore into him now. "So tell me: what's it like playing for your dad?"

The question caught Mickey by surprise. At first he felt a little deflated. So she didn't call just because of my charm and good looks?

But, actually, he'd been thinking a lot about the subject lately. Especially since a certain flame-throwing pitcher who thought he was the greatest thing in the world had joined the Orioles and Mickey and his dad didn't seem to be on the same page anymore.

Oh, it had been nice to see his dad finally crack the whip on Zoom's King Dork behavior the other day. But who knew if that would continue? Would his dad look the other way the next time Zoom went into megajerk mode, pissing off the rest of the team again just when the championship was in their sights?

"There are good things and bad things about playing for your dad," Mickey began. "You get to spend a lot of time with him, which is great. There's always someone to talk to about the games and give you tips and answer your questions. And you know he really cares about you."

He frowned. "What's bad is that sometimes your dad can be too hard on you," he went on. "He has to prove he's treating his kid just like every other player on the team, but sometimes he goes overboard with that.

"And sometimes when you have a bad game, you just want to go home and forget about it. But he wants to talk about it on the car ride home, or at dinner, or while you do homework or whatever. And you're like, 'Dad, give it a rest! My head's about to explode!'"

Abby chuckled softly.

"Oh, and one more thing," Mickey said. "Sometimes the

other players will get mad at you for something your dad did. Like maybe he batted a kid eighth and the kid thinks he should be leading off or something. So he'll complain to you, instead of going to your dad.

"Or if your dad schedules an early-morning practice, the other kids will be like, 'Dude, your dad is wack with this eight a.m. stuff! You gotta talk to him!'"

When he was finished, Abby sighed and looked away. For a moment she seemed lost in thought.

"Guess I'll tell my dad we'll try this coach-daughter thing and see what happens," she said finally. She looked at Mickey and smiled. "You were sweet to come down and talk."

They went back to the stand. It was getting hotter now. The sun was climbing higher in the sky and the dark, threatening clouds of early morning had largely disappeared.

"Let me get you a snowball," she said, "as a little thank-you. This one's on me."

She walked behind the counter and asked, "What flavor are we having today? Oops, never mind. Dumb question."

She grabbed a paper cup, filled it with shaved ice, and moved toward the grape syrup.

"Well," Mickey said nonchalantly, "I thought I might try a Cappuccino Blast today. Or maybe a Key Lime Pie. Or even a Strawberry Shortcake . . ."

Abby's eyes widened.

"Star, you're shocking me!" she said. "But I'm proud of you. Broadening your horizons, expanding your palate. Leaving the wading pool of snowball flavors, so to speak, for the more sophisticated offerings in the deep end."

Mickey nodded happily.

"And after really, *really* thinking it over," he continued, "I think I'm going to go with . . . grape."

Abby stared at him and shook her head in mock sorrow.

"I don't know what I'm going to do with you," she said. "I really don't."

Two days later, four of the Orioles were playing basketball at Smith Clove Park, enjoying their relative freedom before school started again in a few weeks. Even though it was one of those rare summer mornings without oppressive humidity, Mickey was steaming.

This was because the teams were Mickey and Katelyn against Gabe and Sammy, and Sammy was guarding him.

Hacking him unmercifully was the better way to put it.

"I don't know whether you actually know this," Mickey barked, "but when your man beats you to the basket, you're not technically allowed to stop him by grabbing his shorts and giving him a wedgie."

"Yeah, nerd," Katelyn said, glaring at Sammy. "Try that on me and I'll hit you so hard, you'll be spitting teeth for a week."

"And when your man goes in for a layup," Mickey continued, "you can't just bear-hug him. I'm pretty sure that's called a foul."

Sammy wiped the sweat from his forehead and grunted.

"What can I say? I'm not hung up on the rule book. I'm a physical player."

"No, you're a *dirty* player," Mickey said. "Because when you're not grabbing my shorts or bear-hugging me, you're elbowing me in the chest. Or trying to trip me. I'm surprised you haven't hit me with a shovel."

"Picky, picky, picky," Gabe said. "You and K need to man up and stop the whining."

He traded fist bumps with Sammy, the two of them grinning.

"Look at the boy," Gabe said, draping an arm around his teammate. "He's playing his heart out on defense. Does he occasionally get a little out of control? Maybe. Does his game have all the finesse of a hockey goon on a case of Red Bull? Sure. But look at that face."

On cue, Sammy smiled angelically.

"See?" Gabe said. "The boy wouldn't hurt a fly. All he wants to do is get a little exercise. And be with his best friends on this beautiful day."

"Oh, please," Katelyn said, rolling her eyes. "It's definitely time for a break. Before I hurl right here."

As they headed for the water fountain, they saw Hunter sprinting down the hill, shouting and waving at them.

"Why can't he run the base paths that fast?" Gabe said as they watched the little third baseman approach.

"Mainly 'cause he's batting .210 and never *gets* on base," Sammy said, the two of them chuckling.

Hunter reached the court and collapsed on one of the benches.

"You're not gonna believe this," he said, gasping for breath. "Oh, this is good. Really, really good."

He pulled a crumpled piece of paper from his back pocket.

"My mom was on the *Baltimore Sun* Web site and saw this," he said. "Looks like our boy is a genuine . . . no, I don't want to spoil it. Here's the printout. See for yourself."

He thrust the paper at Mickey, who smoothed it and proceeded to read aloud:

"'Police and paramedics credited the quick thinking of a local youth with saving the life of a Pennsylvania woman in a crowded Towson restaurant Thursday.

"'Barbara Perconetti, fifty-two, of Scranton, was having lunch at Eddie's Char-Broil Grill when she began choking on a piece of steak lodged in her throat. When he saw her in distress, a boy at a nearby table jumped up and immediately began performing the Heimlich maneuver on Perconetti, who had begun to turn blue. The choking victim's airway was quickly cleared and she resumed normal breathing.

"'The boy was identified as twelve-year-old'"—here Mickey's eyes nearly popped out of his head—"'Zach Winslow, who will enter eighth grade at York Middle School in the fall.'"

"Whaaat?" Sammy said. "Zoom? A freaking hero?"

"No way!" Katelyn said. "What did he do? Stop her from choking, then push her down a flight of stairs?"

"Wonder if he bragged about the Elite Arms Camp when he was doing the Heimlich on her," Sammy said.

"I'm surprised he didn't have his entourage do it for him," Katelyn said.

As the two of them cracked up and slapped hands, Mickey continued to read:

"'"It was a scary experience—I'm still shaking," Perconnetti told reporters. "But this was the kindest young man I have ever been around. He kept assuring me that everything would be all right. Even after I started breathing again, he stayed and comforted me until the emergency personnel arrived."'"

"The kindest young man?!" Sammy said. "Are we talking about the same Zoom here?"

Katelyn groaned. "Please don't tell me they're giving him some kind of stupid medal," she said.

Mickey pointed at her and said, "We have a win-ah! Give that girl a prize."

He went on reading:

"'Zach will be honored at a special ceremony next month at the Towson fire station, when he will be presented with a framed certificate for his heroism and the Citizens Medal of Honor.

"'"It takes an extraordinary individual to leap into action in the midst of a crisis like that," Fire Captain Pat O'Malley said. "My hat is off to this courageous young man. He's a lifesaver in the truest sense of the word. The entire community should be proud to have him in our midst."'"

When Mickey was finished, the Orioles sat in stunned silence.

"Zoom as a Heimlich knight in shining armor," Katelyn said finally, shaking her head. "I can't believe it."

"Maybe it's like in the movies," Hunter said, "and the guy has a secret split personality! Like with Dr. Jekyll and Mr.

Hyde. Maybe there's a Good Zoom/Bad Zoom thing going on here."

"Maybe. But all we've seen so far is the Jerk Zoom/Jerk Zoom thing," Sammy said as the others nodded.

A moment later, Mickey picked up the basketball and dribbled back out to the court.

"Ladies and gentlemen," he intoned in a dramatic announcer's voice, "we now return you to the second half of the hack-fest, starring our good friend Sammy Noah."

Sammy grinned and shot his hands in the air. Then he ran over to Mickey, dropped into a defensive stance, and hissed, "On you like white on rice, dude."

Even as the game started up again, Mickey couldn't stop thinking about Zoom.

Here was a kid who had seemed like nothing but a spoiled, egotistical brat who cared only about making himself look good.

Yet according to the newspaper article, he had rushed in selflessly to help a stranger in distress and shown extraordinary kindness to the shaken woman before it was all over.

What is the deal with you, Zoom Winslow? Mickey found himself wondering.

Was there something else to the kid besides the ever-present scowl and arrogant attitude that had turned the rest of the Orioles against him?

And—again—why didn't the kid ever seem like he was having any fun playing baseball? Especially when he had all that talent?

Mickey was still dying to know.

But he didn't seem any closer to the answers.

18

Mickey was no psychologist, but he could sense intuitively right before a big game whether his team was ready to play or not. And in the moments before the Orioles took the field against the Twins, he knew the mood in the O's dugout was all wrong.

You didn't want to see players so loose that everyone was just joking around and not warming up properly and not concentrating. But you also didn't want them so tight that they looked ready to crack, each player worriedly running through what his dad called "what-if scenarios":

What if I strike out with the bases loaded?

What if I drop a fly ball in a critical situation?

What if I just plain suck today and it costs us the game? And maybe the championship?

Right now, Mickey sensed, that's where the Orioles were mentally, deep in the dark jungle of *what if?* With no clue how to hack their way out.

The noise level in the dugout? Crickets. It was as if someone had just died. The only thing missing was the corpse.

He looked down the bench. Katelyn sat silently with

her glove in her lap, rocking back and forth. Mickey had never seen her this quiet before a game. Usually, she was the one walking up and down the dugout, firing everyone up, spouting wisecracks and trash talk and vowing to personally destroy the other team with a superhuman 4-for-4, two-homer night.

Sammy was nervously stuffing handfuls of sunflower seeds into his mouth and spitting out shells like a machine gun. Corey and Ethan tossed a ball between them listlessly, until Corey waved his hand and barked, "Stop! You're driving me crazy!"

Hunter had already leaped off the bench and gone to the men's room three times in the past ten minutes, a sure sign of major jitters.

Even Gabe looked tense, chomping furiously on his bubble gum and staring out at the field as the Twins finished infield practice.

Then there was Zoom.

As usual, the kid had arrived about fifteen minutes before game time, strutting up to the field with his boys, each of them sucking noisily on huge sodas. A few of the Orioles, who had just heard about his lifesaving role in the restaurant—a local TV station had picked up the story and was now calling him "The Heimlich Hero"—had clapped him on the back and offered congratulations.

But Zoom had simply shrugged and warmed up quickly, throwing alongside Danny, who liked to loosen his arm early, even though he was the late-inning reliever.

Now, however, Zoom sat alone in his usual spot at the end of the bench. His face shone with a thin sheen of perspiration, despite it being another relatively cool night, and his feet jiggled incessantly.

Apparently, the big-game pressure was getting to him, too.

This is crazy, Mickey thought. There's no life here. No confidence. We'll lose by ten runs if we come out this tense. Somebody has to say something!

He was about to jump to his feet when his dad clambered down the steps.

"All right, listen up. Here's the batting order," he began. He ticked off the usual names and positions and then paused. ". . . And Danny will be starting on the mound."

There was a collective gasp.

No one moved. It seemed as if no one was even breathing now. The rest of the players cut furtive glances at Zoom and Danny.

Zoom's jaw dropped and he stared wide-eyed at Coach. It was the first time Mickey had seen him without either a frown or a smug look.

Meanwhile, all the color had drained from Danny's face.

"Uh, Coach," Danny stammered at last, "do you really think that's a good idea? This is, you know, such a, um, big game and all. And me starting, well, I—"

Mickey's dad cut him off with a dismissive wave.

"You'll do fine, Danny," he said. "We have a lot of confidence in you. All right, let's take the field. Important game, sure. But go out there and have fun, people."

Mickey was so shocked that it took him a few seconds to process what his dad had said. He grabbed his mask and glove and turned for one last look at Zoom.

Slowly, the boy lowered his head and covered his face in his hands.

Never thought I'd see the day, Mickey thought. He's going to break down and cry. Bet it'll be the Niagara Falls of tears, too.

But when Zoom looked up again, Mickey saw that he was wrong.

There were no tears. Instead, Zoom's jaw was clenched and his eyes were twin dark slits. He shot a murderous glare at Coach, who had his back turned as he taped the lineup to the dugout wall. Then Zoom draped a towel over his head, folded his arms, and stared straight ahead.

Guess Dad has finally had it with *all* of Zoom's antics, Mickey thought, not just the crazy *Z* slashes after the strikeouts.

But to bench him in a game with so much on the line . . .

There was no time to think about that now. Mickey needed to get Danny ready to go.

And Danny was a basket case.

He sailed the first two warm-up pitches over Mickey's head. The third one bounced ten feet in front of the plate. Mickey jogged out to the mound.

"Okay, I'm no expert at this," he began, hoping to get Danny to smile and relax, "but it seems like your control might be off a tiny bit."

It didn't work. Danny was even paler now. He licked his lips nervously.

"*You* know I'm not a starter!" he hissed, slamming the ball into his glove. "*I* know I'm not a starter. What's wrong with your crazy dad?"

Mickey put a hand on his shoulder.

"You can do this," Mickey said. "Ever hear the story about Justin Verlander's first start for the Detroit Tigers?"

"*Stories?!*" Danny squeaked. "We have time for stories now?"

"It's a quick one," Mickey said. "Verlander was so nervous he could hardly grip the ball. The pitching coach came out and told him to imagine every batter naked. It helped calm him down right away."

Danny looked horrified.

"*Ewww!*" he said. He glanced at the Twins lead-off batter, a short, chunky kid taking warm-up swings in the on-deck circle, and shook his head. "You want me to imagine that dude with no clothes on? That's the sickest thing I ever heard in my life!"

"Maybe," Mickey said, "but it worked. All of a sudden Verlander wasn't worried about getting the ball over the plate."

"*Seriously?*" Danny said. "That's the best you got? Picture the batter *naked*? Well, that's not gonna happen."

Mickey shrugged. "Fine, it's unconventional. You want conventional? Take a couple of deep breaths and relax."

But Danny couldn't do that, either.

He walked the first two Twins batters, then was so rattled that he took five miles per hour off his fastball and started aiming his pitches. The result was predictable: Yanni Mendez, the Twins best hitter, drove a two-run double to left. And the next kid up hit a single up the middle to score Yanni.

Danny finally settled down, striking out the next two

batters and getting the number eight hitter on a weak comebacker to the mound. But the damage was done.

Twins 3, Orioles 0.

When he jogged off the mound, Danny headed straight for Mickey, wagging his finger.

"Thanks for totally messing me up," he said. "I couldn't even concentrate out there. All I could think of was those guys naked."

Overhearing this, Katelyn whirled around and stared at Danny.

"Nerd, that is *so* totally gross!" she said. "Are you like some kind of sicko perv?"

With that, she took off her cap and smacked him over the head with it before walking away. Danny started to protest, then shook his head sadly and sat down. Mickey stifled a laugh.

This would be hysterical, he thought, if we weren't getting our butts beat.

But the Orioles came right back in the third inning when the Twins pitcher, Billy Adelman, began having his own control problems. He walked Ethan, the lead-off batter, and followed with another walk to Justin. Then he promptly drilled Danny in the left shoulder to load the bases.

"Serves the little sicko right," Katelyn muttered as Danny jogged to first, rubbing his new bruise.

Hunter followed with a clutch two-run single that had the Orioles on their feet and whooping. Katelyn popped out to the third baseman and Sammy struck out on a nasty curve by Billy. But Mickey followed with a sharp single to left and decided to try for second when he saw the left fielder bobble the ball momentarily.

He made it in safely with a showy pop-up slide, then smiled and pumped his fist. The Orioles dugout was a sea of noise now, everyone up on the top step, whooping and slapping hands and chanting, "MICK-EE! MICK-EE!"

Well, not everyone. One kid was conspicuously absent from all the celebration. And that kid sat at the end of the bench with his arms crossed and a towel over his head, glowering.

Sorry, Zoom, Mickey thought. This time it's not all about you.

It was still 3–3 in the fourth inning, the Orioles coming to bat, when Zoom suddenly rose and began stretching his shoulder and windmilling his arm.

The rest of the Orioles watched him and nodded to one another.

The unspoken thoughts rippling through all of them were: Good. Zoom's coming in to lock this baby up. Danny's looking shaky again. Good move by Coach. He taught Zoom a lesson—sure, a powerful lesson—about the need to be a better teammate and not be such a jerk.

But now it was time to bring the heat and win this game.

Mickey's dad watched Zoom impassively for a few seconds.

Then he looked down the bench and said, "Sammy, go warm up. You're coming in for Danny."

It was hard to tell who was more stunned, Sammy or Zoom or the rest of the Orioles.

Sammy hadn't pitched since the third game of the season, when Danny was home sick and Sammy had to come on in relief of Gabe. Now he was looking at Coach as if to say, *You're kidding, right? This is all a joke?*

Zoom seemed even more confused. Slowly, he sank back on the bench and let out a low moan. He leaned forward and buried his face in his hands again.

But this time when he looked up, all the rage and defiance were gone.

This time there *were* tears streaming down his face.

Sammy recovered quickly from his shock. After all, everyone on the team—including him—knew he was the logical choice to pitch if Zoom wasn't coming in. Sammy had the strongest arm of any of the fielders, for one thing. And he wasn't shy about showing it off.

How often had the Orioles seen him range far to his left at shortstop to backhand a grounder, plant his back foot like he was stomping on an anthill, then gun a throw across the diamond to get the base runner?

There were times Mickey swore that Sammy held the ball a second or two longer on those plays than he had to, just to make the throw to first more of a challenge, to see if he could still nip the runner after silently counting, *One Mississippi, two Mississippi . . .*

Sammy always insisted he never did that. But Mickey didn't believe him.

The only reason Sammy didn't pitch more often for the Orioles was that he happened to be the best short-stop in the league. "If it ain't broke, don't fix it," Mickey's dad always said. He wasn't about to tinker with a kid who seemed genetically engineered to play the position.

The other thing about Sammy that made him the right choice to pitch was this: he didn't rattle easily.

Even now he seemed relatively calm as he stood on the mound and listened to Mickey go over the strategy for the next two innings.

"I don't think you should throw your curve," Mickey said.

"Good," Sammy said. "Because I don't have a curve."

"I remember you had sort of a curve," Mickey said.

"*Sort* of a curve?" Sammy said. "Do we really want to throw that in a game like this?"

"Fine," Mickey said. "Just stick to your fastball. And mix in the changeup, all right?"

"Well," Sammy said, "there's a problem there, too."

Mickey said, "Let me guess. You don't have a changeup, either."

Sammy nodded. "And this is no time to experiment with *sort* of a changeup. Not against these guys. It'll end up in the next county."

"Ohhh-kay," Mickey said. "Guess we'll go with all fast-balls, then."

Sammy grinned and rubbed up the ball. "Sounds like a plan."

The plan got the Orioles through the fifth inning unscathed.

Sammy wasn't a good enough pitcher to blow batters away, even with his powerful arm. There was a vast differ-ence between making throws from short and consistently firing the ball over the plate when the game was on the line and a batter was glaring at you.

But Sammy threw hard enough—and was just wild enough—that the Twins batters couldn't dig in and tee off, either. And the Orioles defense rose to the occasion.

Corey made a nice running catch of a drive to left-center for the first out. Then Hunter at third base charged a slow roller and scooped it bare-handed before making an off-balance throw to beat the runner at first by a step.

After each nice play, Sammy pointed at his fielders and shouted, "Oh, yeah! Oh, yeah!"

Mickey shook his head in wonder.

What a difference there was between Sammy's infectious enthusiasm and willingness to credit his defense and the way Zoom seemed to regard everyone who played behind him as more of a pain in the butt than anything else.

With his confidence growing, Sammy reached back for something extra on his fastball and he struck out the next batter on four pitches, racing off the mound with a big smile.

The rest of the Orioles greeted him with high fives.

"Pretty good for a guy with one pitch," Mickey said.

Sammy shrugged. "You have to know your limitations."

"And yours are so numerous we couldn't list them all here," Katelyn said. Then she smacked him on the butt and added, "But good work out there, nerd."

As she walked away, Sammy said, "I . . . *think* that was a compliment."

"Or as close as you're going to get from her," Mickey said.

"Know what would really help now?" Sammy said, reaching for his water bottle. "If we could score some runs. Having a cushion would be nice for Mr. One Pitch."

"Working on it," Mickey said. "Problem is, our bats aren't cooperating. Or maybe it's their pitchers."

The Orioles failed to score in their half of the fifth, as the pitcher who came on in relief of Billy Adelman turned out to have a mediocre fastball, but a mesmerizing curveball—when he could actually get it over the plate. But the Orioles were so anxious they were overswinging, and the kid set them down in order.

Sammy did his job again, and so did the Orioles defense. The Twins cleanup hitter led off with a single, but Mickey gunned him down at second when he tried to steal. The next batter popped out to Hunter in foul territory. And Corey raced in to make a shoestring catch off a fly ball to center field for the third out.

This time, Sammy pumped his fist as he sprinted to the dugout. Seeing his excitement seemed to fire up the rest of the Orioles. They were down to their last three outs— at least if they wanted to avoid extra innings. But Mickey could sense that they were determined not to blow this chance at the win.

"All right, everybody listen up," Coach said. But the Orioles already knew exactly where this little speech was going. They had heard it before—many times.

"Let's be patient up there," Coach began.

"Translation: somebody draw a walk and get on base," Hunter whispered.

"Wait for your pitch," Coach said.

"Which, ideally, would be ball four," Katelyn murmured.

"And remember," Coach said, "a walk's as good as a hit."

"Ahh!" Ethan said. "We arrive at the crux of the matter."

But the Orioles didn't have to be patient. Right away, it was obvious the Twins pitcher was struggling with his control. He caught Ethan on the elbow with a curveball that didn't quite curve. And one batter later, he threw the same pitch to Justin, who took it on his hip.

Just like that, the Orioles had runners on first and second with no outs. The Twins pitcher looked rattled, stalking around the mound red-faced and mumbling to himself. The Twins coach quickly called time to try to settle the boy down, but now the kid just barked at him.

"You can talk to him all you want, Coach," Gabe said gleefully, "but that kid is done. Stick a fork in him. You can read it in his body language. He'll be lucky if he can throw another strike."

He didn't. On a 2–0 count, Sammy reached for a fastball well off the plate and slapped a single to right field. Ethan chugged around from second with the winning run.

Final score: Orioles 4, Twins 3.

While the Twins trudged disconsolately off the field, the Orioles raced from their dugout, mobbing Ethan and Sammy and slapping hands with one another.

As Mickey joined in the celebration, he saw Abby standing near the backstop, clapping and giving him the thumbs-up sign. Something else in the backdrop of happy faces caught his eye.

Zoom was off to one side, watching it all with a wistful look.

No, Mickey thought, he's not jumping up and down and geeking out with everyone else. But at least he's not racing out to the parking lot with his boys, either.

A moment later, Coach waded into their midst and held up his hands for quiet.

"Got a little news flash for you guys," he said. "Just heard this from one of our parents. Ready? The Indians lost again tonight."

It took a second or two for the Orioles to process his words. Then they erupted in more whoops and cheers.

Now the last game of the regular season would be for the championship.

It would be Orioles vs. Indians, winner goes on to play the team with the biggest, baddest rep in the whole area.

"How sweet would that be?" Mickey found himself saying. He could see the preening Huntington Yankees now, with their gleaming new unis and shiny new bats and gloves, and their arrogant coach and his spoiled-brat kid, thinking they were the greatest team ever, God's gift to youth baseball and . . .

Then he caught himself.

What were those old clichés his dad was always spouting? About playing 'em one game at a time, never looking past your next opponent, and blah, blah, blah?

Mickey knew his dad was right.

But it sure was hard to do now.

20

It was the next day and Mickey and his dad were cooking dinner on the back deck. His mom was away on a business trip. Mickey dropped a chunk of ground beef on the grill that landed with a thud. It sizzled and sent a thin plume of smoke billowing into the air.

His dad watched him for a moment, then asked, "What do you call that . . . *thing*?"

"What thing?" Mickey said.

He reached for the spatula and tried to flip the meat. But it was so big that it fell off, breaking into several pieces. Mickey fit the pink lumps together as best he could with his fingers and pushed the whole mess toward the flames.

"I'm talking about that *thing* you're grilling," his dad said.

"This?" Mickey said, patting the meat lovingly with the spatula. "It's a burger."

"No, that's not *a* burger," his dad said. "That's like, I don't know, *four* burgers. All mushed together into one big . . . *blob*. Is there a name for that? Look at it! It's the size of a manhole cover, for God's sake!"

Mickey nodded happily.

"I was going more for a bowling-ball look," he said. "But, okay, 'manhole cover' works."

He stabbed at the meat with the spatula again and this time managed to flip it.

"You're what, twelve?" his dad said with a grin. "You'll have the cholesterol level of a sixty-year-old if you eat that. So will I, come to think of it. And I'm only thirty-eight. Although I'd like to live to be thirty-nine, thank you."

He gazed at the burger crackling on the fire and shook his head. "Your mother would freak out if she saw all that meat."

Mickey draped an arm around his dad and looked around furtively. He dropped his voice to a conspiratorial whisper.

"Thing is, Mom's not here, Dad," he said. "Which means she doesn't have to know. It's like I always say: 'What happens at the grill stays at the grill.'"

The two of them laughed so hard that tears came to Mickey's eyes, though the smoke from the grill could have contributed, too.

For as long as Mickey could remember, his dad had let him watch when he grilled on summer evenings. Finally, a year or so ago, Mickey had graduated to working over the hot flames himself, which basically consisted of firing up the biggest, fattest burgers anyone had ever seen.

He threw another ball of beef on the fire and sighed contentedly. The sun was going down and a cool breeze was rippling through the backyard, tinkling the wind chimes and rustling the flowers in the garden.

The two of them sat in silence for a moment. Then his dad took a sip of his iced tea and said, "I have a feeling you have a question or two about last night's game."

Oh, yeah, Mickey thought. Once again it was as if his dad had read his mind.

They had arrived home late after the big win over the Twins—and an obligatory stop at Abby's snowball stand—and both of them had been too tired to review the game on the car ride home.

Mickey had gone to bed early, and by the time he climbed out of bed in the morning, his dad had already left for a weekend meeting at the insurance agency.

This was the first time the two of them had had a moment to talk about the crazy events of twenty-four hours earlier.

"Think I was too hard on Zoom?" his dad asked.

Mickey shrugged and thought for a moment.

"No, I don't think so," he said at last.

His dad grunted. "I don't know. I kind of feel like I blew it with that kid. Gabe got hurt, and I saw all that talent in Zoom, and I just sort of . . . lost my mind. The first time I saw the kid pitch, I thought, 'That arm is our ticket to winning the whole league.' And I let myself be blinded by that desire."

He took another sip of iced tea. "All of a sudden I was letting him do things I'd never let any other player do: show up late for games, call his own pitches, disrespect his teammates, dream up crazy plays to make himself look better."

Mickey cocked an eyebrow. He'd never said a word to

his dad about Zoom's pickoff stunt—not even to Gabe. Someone else on the team must have ratted on Zoom. But who?

Mickey flipped the burgers and went back to listening with rapt attention.

"I just kept telling myself, 'Oh, give him a break, he's new, he'll get with the program pretty soon,'" his dad continued. "Ha! It wasn't fair to you and it wasn't fair to the rest of the team. It wasn't fair to Zoom, either. He's just a kid! How can he learn to be a good teammate when his dumb coach is putting him on a pedestal and letting him do whatever he wants!"

His dad rubbed his eyes wearily.

"The more I let him get away with, the more he tested me, tested the boundaries. You guys all saw that, I'm sure. But for some stupid reason, I didn't. Then finally, when he struck out that kid in the Rays game and tried to embarrass him with that Z-slash stuff, it was like the light came on for me.

"I was horrified! It was like I had created this *monster*! Or *helped* create him, anyway."

The burgers were finally done. Mickey scooped them off the grill and onto a plate. He grabbed another platter with all the fixings, and he and his dad sat at a patio table.

"You go ahead and eat, buddy," his dad said softly. "I don't have much of an appetite all of a sudden."

Mickey couldn't remember ever seeing his dad beat himself up about a decision he'd made. On the other hand, his dad had never had to deal with this kind of head-case talent before.

"What happens with Zoom now?" Mickey asked.

"Well, if he comes back to the team with the same arrogance and disregard for his teammates, he won't play," his dad said. "If he comes back with a different attitude and realizes the team comes first, he'll pitch for us again. It's that simple. And it's up to him."

He drained the last of his iced tea and sighed.

"But, heck, he might not come back at all! He might decide I'm the worst coach in the world and the biggest jerk he ever played for. He might just say, 'I am *so-o-o* done with the Orioles.' "

Mickey nodded as he reached for a roll. "He *was* pretty upset over being benched," he said. "He had tears in his eyes when you put Sammy in."

"Yeah, I saw that," his dad said. "I felt bad for the kid. I really did. But he has to learn a lesson here. Guess we'll find out next week when we play the Indians. *If* he shows up. . . ."

Now it was Mickey who was down, who felt things unraveling. The thought of not having Zoom on the mound against the Indians gave him a sinking feeling. Even if the Orioles somehow managed to win without Zoom, they'd get totally destroyed by the Huntington Yankees the following week.

Danny would get lit up like a refinery fire by that power-packed lineup. So, probably, would Sammy. Or anyone else they threw at those studs.

Okay, Mickey told himself, gotta get out of this negative mood. Can't have both me and Dad down in the dumps. Maybe some food will help. Sure, that always does the trick.

Slowly and methodically, he began building his burger with all the ritual of a priest preparing Communion.

First he placed the burger exactly in the middle of the roll.

Next he placed a slice of cheese on top, making sure the four corners hung over the burger just so.

After that he added two slices of lettuce, followed by a slice of tomato and a slice of onion.

He was just beginning to add pickles, arranged in a concentric pattern with two on top, two on the bottom and one in the middle, when he sensed his dad staring at him.

Looking up, he saw a smile beginning to form on the corners of his dad's mouth.

"What?" Mickey said, holding up the burger. "It's a work of art. You can't rush greatness."

"Apparently not," his dad said. "But by the time that work of art is ready to eat, it'll be time for bed."

It was good to see his dad's gloom starting to lift. It made Mickey feel better, too.

As dusk settled in around them and he began chomping on his newest culinary creation, he was consumed with two questions:

Number one, would Zoom, the best pitcher he'd ever seen, ever play for the Orioles again?

And number two, did his dad want that other burger?

Or was that baby officially up for grabs?

Abby sent the pitch from Mickey crashing into the left-field fence on one bounce. It hit with a loud *WHAP!* and careened a good ten feet to the right—a sure double if she were running it out in a real game.

Standing on the pitcher's mound, Mickey gave a low, admiring whistle as he fished another softball from the duffel bag at his feet.

"You got good wood on that one," he said. "Or maybe *good composite*'s the better term. At least with that bat."

Abby winced and stepped out of the batter's box.

"*Good composite* doesn't sound right, star," she said. "It's like you're complimenting me for developing a new fiber-reinforced polymer or something."

"A new fiber reinforced *what?*" Mickey asked.

"Sorry," Abby said sheepishly. "My mom's an industrial chemist."

"Oh," Mickey said with a grin. "Then I should have picked up on that. 'Cause I hang with industrial chemists all the time."

Abby threw her head back and laughed, which Mickey

found absolutely thrilling. He hadn't seen her laugh that hard since that day he'd spotted her talking to Zoom at the snowball stand, when Zoom had probably told her a dumb joke or something.

Maybe, Mickey hoped now, that had been a pity laugh for the new kid. This laugh just now, this was the real deal—Abby's entire face had lit up.

Score one for Michael J. Labriogla, he thought. The kid hits a three-pointer! From way beyond the arc, too!

For the better part of twenty minutes on this humid afternoon, Mickey had been windmilling pitch after pitch to Abby.

It was the result of another phone call to the Labriogla household—an hour earlier, in the middle of the afternoon—from one ELLIOTT, ABBY. Mickey had answered only to be greeted with another no-nonsense, right-to-the-point request:

"Come pitch batting practice for me. I'm in a hitting slump with my softball team. Please? Don't let me down. You can help change a life, Mickey."

How could he refuse an offer like that?

This time he was out the door and on his bike in approximately fifteen seconds, practically fishtailing down the road like they did in those car-chase scenes in the movies.

In the process, he'd almost run over an old man carrying groceries and a mom pushing a baby stroller, both of whom had looked terrified at the sight of this wild-eyed, red-haired, freckle-faced vision of death careening toward them on the sidewalk.

Now, with his shirt soaked with sweat from having

thrown some forty pitches and jogging after countless batted balls all over the field, Mickey had arrived at two conclusions:

First, the girl could hit. Abby was barely five feet tall, with the slender arms and thin wrists of a ballerina. But she stepped forcefully into each pitch and had one of the smoothest swings Mickey had ever seen, the ball seeming to jump off her bat.

And second, his arm was starting to throb. Actually, it was way beyond throbbing—it was practically screaming in agony. Maybe it was because windmilling a softball didn't come easily to him. And he wasn't very good at it, either.

Actually, he had to admit, he just plain sucked at it.

Of the forty or so pitches he'd thrown, only about twenty had been anywhere near the strike zone. Luckily, Abby hadn't rolled her eyes at this futility or directed any snide remarks his way, which Mickey would have done in a heartbeat if the roles had been reversed.

But whatever the secret was to snapping off a pitch underhand and getting it over the plate, he was completely clueless.

"Can we take a break now?" Mickey asked, rubbing his shoulder.

In the next instant he thought: Did that come out as too whiny? God, I hope not. Don't want to seem like a wimp out here. If Gabe heard me just then, he'd be all over me about it for weeks.

"One more pitch," Abby said.

She stepped out again and pointed her bat dramatically at the outfield fence.

"Really?" Mickey said, shaking his head. "You're calling this shot, Babe Ruth–style?"

"Calling it," Abby said, grinning.

She dug in again, holding the bat high and waving it in tiny, menacing circles. "Just give me something I can hit, star."

Actually, it took four more pitches before he put one over the plate. Abby swung ferociously, but she got under the ball and hit a lazy pop-up that Mickey gloved easily on the first-base side of the mound.

"Oh, wait a minute," he said innocently. "Were you calling a weak little infield flare? I'm sorry; I thought you were calling a home run. My bad."

Abby tossed her bat in disgust. Then, to Mickey's great relief—he wasn't sure how she'd handle sarcasm at the moment—she managed a smile.

"You're on a roll today with the jokes," she said. "You really are."

They got a drink at the water fountain and collapsed in the shade under a nearby oak tree.

"So how's it going with your dad coaching your softball team?" Mickey asked.

"No problems at all," Abby said, chuckling. "I told him: 'As long as you let me bat cleanup and play any position I want and never take me out of the game, we'll get along just fine.'"

Mickey laughed. "Maybe I'll try that with my dad. Bet that would go over real well."

"Seriously, my dad's only coached two games," Abby said. "And we won both of them, even though his daughter's in the Grand Canyon of all batting slumps. But so far, it's been fun having him running the team."

Suddenly her face clouded over.

"I'm more worried about *your* team, star," she said. "No Zoom on the mound the last game—what was *that* all about?"

Briefly, Mickey explained the reasons for Zoom's benching, starting with his tardiness at games and general it's-all-about-me attitude, and culminating with the infamous Z-slash strikeout celebration that had already become the talk of the league.

When he was through, Abby nodded and said, "Okay, that explains his texts."

"Explains what?" Mickey said.

"Why Zoom has seemed so . . . *different* the last couple of days," Abby said. "He's been texting me a lot—again."

Instantly, Mickey could feel his irritation flame on again. The guy's killing me, he thought. Plus I gotta get a cell phone—real fast.

"How did he seem different?" he asked.

"Know how he's always bragging about himself?" Abby said. "Talking about Elite Arms Camp, how no one can hit him, how he's the greatest and all that stuff? This time there was none of that."

Mickey nodded. "The boy's been humbled. My dad kind of owned him up for being a jerk."

"Well," Abby said, "Zoom didn't mention any of that. He just seemed, I don't know . . . down. He even said he's getting tired of baseball. He isn't sure he wants to play it anymore."

"He *said* that?"

"I told him that was crazy talk," Abby said. "I told him with that arm and all that talent, he should love baseball more than any other kid on the planet."

"What did he say to that?"

Abby shrugged. "He didn't text me after that." She wore a worried frown. "You guys really *need* him against the Indians, too."

Mickey tried to envision Danny going up against the Indians' strong lineup—steady, crafty Danny, but with a fastball that scared nobody. Even Sammy with his strong arm could be in for trouble, with no curve or changeup to keep the hitters off balance.

By the second or third inning, the Indians could be timing his pitches and *raking.*

Raking like it was batting practice.

Then Mickey caught himself. Dude, he thought, what's with all the negativity again? All the gloom and doom? This was no time to get down and lose confidence.

What was the expression his mom used? "No time to go all wobbly"? Even without Zoom, the Orioles were a good, solid team. They'd do just fine against the Indians.

Maybe they'd even be better off without him. Happier and more cohesive, like when Sammy was pitching. As for Mickey himself, he wouldn't exactly mind if the pitcher never graced Abby's snowball stand again.

To break the mood, he picked up Abby's bat and held the knob in front of him like it was a microphone.

In a theatrical broadcaster's voice, he thundered, "So it all comes down to this, sports fans: one game, Orioles versus Indians, with a season on the line! And from what we've seen of these young, scrappy Orioles, they're certainly up to the challenge, no matter who takes the mound for them!"

Abby laughed and wagged a finger at him.

"Hate to remind you of this, Mr. Announcer Guy," she said, "but the Indians are a pretty good team."

"So are the Orioles, young lady," Mickey intoned, still in full sportscaster mode. "They've battled back from adversity all year long. And this Friday evening, in the cozy confines of Eddie Murray Field, the two teams will settle the question of who's best once and for all. Tickets are going fast, folks. So don't miss this epic matchup, brought to you by McDonald's! 'I'm Loving It!' And by Toyota, 'Let's Go Places!' And by—"

"Okay," Abby interrupted, "now you're starting to scare me. Anyone ever tell you you're watching *way* too much sports on TV? Or way too many commercials, anyway."

Now they were both chuckling. But Mickey had to admit he was feeling better about the Orioles' chances if Zoom didn't show up Friday.

He hoped this wasn't the baseball equivalent of whistling past the graveyard.

If it was, the season could be over real soon.

One of the things Mickey loved most about game days was the ride to the field with his dad.

Usually it was just the two of them talking about the team they were about to face and going over strategy: what to do against the opposing pitcher, how to pitch to this kid and that kid, what to do if the other team got cute and decided to make it a track meet on the bases and test Mickey's arm.

Mickey never felt closer to his dad than when they talked baseball in their ancient minivan, which was the size of an army tank and apparently just as indestructible. As they drove to Eddie Murray Field to play the Indians, the only thing spoiling the trip was an annoying *tap-tap-tap* coming from the floorboards.

Finally, his dad asked, "Okay, why so nervous?"

"Me?" Mickey said. "I'm not nervous."

"You're not nervous?"

"Nope," Mickey said. "Why?"

"Oh, no reason," his dad said. "Just that you've been tapping your feet nonstop since we left home. You don't hear that? It's so loud, at first I thought we had a flat tire."

Mickey looked down. Sure enough, his sneakers were beating a staccato rhythm on the floor mats.

Somehow he willed his legs to stay still.

"Sorry," he said sheepishly. "Just . . . thinking about the game, I guess."

His dad smiled and patted Mickey's shoulder.

"Relax," he said. "We'll do just fine. No matter who pitches."

Maybe, Mickey thought. But much of the earlier optimism he'd felt about the Orioles' chances against the Indians was beginning to disappear.

For one thing, there was the inconvenient fact that the O's had lost to the Indians in a 10–8 slugfest earlier in the season, even though Gabe had pitched a pretty good game. And thinking about the Indians' hard-hitting lineup—a bunch of "big, hairy-knuckled guys," as his dad had called them—Mickey remembered they were also patient at the plate, refusing to swing at bad pitches and content to draw walks if that's what it took to get a rally going.

The memories of that game were making him anxious all over again.

Maybe a couple of the big, hairy-knuckled guys are sick tonight, Mickey thought. Or maybe they can't get to the game 'cause their parents' car broke down or something.

The thought of Tyler Hanson, the Indians' feared cleanup hitter, standing forlornly on the side of the road with his mom next to their SUV, with the hood popped and smoke billowing from the engine, made him chuckle grimly.

As usual, Mickey and his dad were the first to arrive at

the ballpark. As his dad went off to check on the condition of the field, Mickey carried the heavy equipment bag to the dugout. Even with the sun starting to go down, the temperature was still in the low nineties and the humidity was rain-forest thick.

"Hot sticky night, catcher's delight," an umpire working the plate had said to him once on a similar evening. And the two of them, sweltering in their face masks, chest protectors, and shin guards, had chuckled at the absurdity of that statement.

Mickey was about to heave the equipment bag onto the bench and go back to get the water bottles when a shadow loomed over his shoulder.

"Hey," a voice said.

Mickey was so startled that he dropped the bag, which crashed to the cement floor, spilling baseballs and bats. He whipped around.

His jaw dropped.

It was Zoom.

"What?" Zoom said. "Don't tell me I'm too early. An hour before game time, right? Isn't that when we're supposed to be here? Or did I screw this one up, too?"

Mickey tried to speak, but all he could do was nod. Just then his dad clambered down the steps.

"Mick," he began, "I need the rake to smooth out that—"

When he spotted Zoom, he froze.

No one spoke for several seconds.

Then Zoom said quietly, "Can you give me another chance?"

Mickey could see it was a completely different Zoom standing before them now.

Gone were the over-the-top swagger and perpetual smirk the Orioles had come to know—and hate. Nor was there the hint of the sulky look he'd break out whenever things weren't going exactly his way, or when people weren't treating him like a young god.

No, this was a humbled kid with a pleading tone and sad-looking eyes.

His dad seemed to study Zoom for a moment.

"Okay," he said finally. "You and Mick go loosen up. We'll see what happens after that."

A look of pure relief came over Zoom's face. He grabbed his glove, clapped Mickey on the back, and yelled, "Yeah! Let's do this!"

Ten minutes later, as the Orioles began trickling in, they seemed puzzled to see Zoom stretching down the third-base line.

"What's he doing here so early?" Sammy asked. "Are all the clocks in his house broken?"

"Doesn't he know this'll ruin his image?" Hunter said. "Next thing you know he'll start showing up on time for practice, too. And from there, who knows where it'll end? He might start winning attendance awards in school."

Mickey had to agree that it was weird seeing Zoom take batting practice and infield with the rest of the team half an hour later. Even weirder was how he was acting. Instead of standing off by himself as he usually did before a game, he was actually talking and laughing with the other Orioles.

When infield was over, Katelyn marched up to Mickey and jabbed a finger in his chest.

"I demand to know what you've done with Zoom, nerd," she said. "And who's this new kid occupying his body?"

Mickey glanced around furtively, then whispered, "It's probably better for you not to know. If I told you, I'd have to kill you."

"I'm serious," Katelyn said. "The boy is actually being friendly. And telling jokes. *Jokes!* And they're funny, too! Here I thought the boy's sense of humor had been removed at birth."

Mickey grinned. "Maybe he was snatched by aliens. And they're such an advanced civilization, they can perform personality transplants."

"There's something else that's weird," Katelyn continued. "Remember that old game 'what's wrong with this picture?'"

"Sure," Mickey said. "One of my all-time favorites."

"Well, look up in the stands," Katelyn said. "Now tell me: what's wrong with this picture?"

Mickey did as he was told. But all he saw was the usual assortment of tired-looking moms and dads, bored grandparents, and amped-up little kids pounding up and down the bleachers.

"I give up," Mickey said. "What's different?"

"See Zoom's posse anywhere?" she said. "You know, the famous Dork Trio? Who've apparently attended every game of his since he was, like, three?"

Mickey looked again. Katelyn was right. He saw Zoom's dad sitting in his usual spot, two rows from the top, all the way to the left, appearing to tinker with his smartphone. But there was no sign of the three solemn, moon-faced kids who composed Zoom's entourage.

"Wow," Mickey said. "Maybe he fired them. Like Jay-Z probably does with his boys three or four times a week."

Fifteen minutes before game time, Mickey's dad beckoned Mickey and Zoom to join him in the dugout.

He pulled a gleaming new baseball from its box and handed it to Zoom.

"Okay," he said. "You're pitching. It's a big game. But you don't worry about that. Just go out there and do your best. And you don't have to strike everyone out. You've got some good fielders behind you. Don't be afraid to use them."

Zoom nodded and exhaled deeply, as if another weight had been lifted from his shoulders.

"Oh, and one more thing," Coach said. "Mickey's going to call the pitches. I'll let you guys go over the signs. But whatever he puts down, that's what you throw. No exceptions. Understood?"

This is it, Mickey thought.

This is when the kid's finally going to flip out. And revert to the spoiled-diva Zoom. The kid who wants everything his way and would rather drive a nail through his eyeball than have the catcher tell him what to throw.

Mickey braced for the whiny protest that was sure to come; the narrowed eyes, the pouty look.

But all Zoom did was murmur, "Got it, Coach." Then to Mickey: "Let's go warm up some more, okay?"

In the moments before the Orioles took the field, Mickey's head was still spinning over Zoom's incredible transformation. It really *was* as if the kid had been beamed aboard a spaceship and sent back to Earth as a completely different person.

But there were still a couple of key questions to be answered.

Could this new and improved version of Zoom pitch like the old Zoom?

Or would the kid with the new choirboy demeanor lose his fire and his fastball and get rocked by the bruisers in the other dugout?

"Guess we're about to find out," Mickey said to himself.

He plopped on the bench and began pulling on his chest protector.

There it was again: that *tap-tap-tap* sound.

He looked down at his feet.

This time he knew where it was coming from.

One look at Zoom's game face helped Mickey relax.

As Zoom stood tall on the mound and peered in for the sign, he held up his glove so all you could see were his eyes, the way the big-league pitchers did for maximum intimidation.

When he went into his windup, uncoiled his right arm, and the first fastball slammed into Mickey's glove for a strike, Zoom had the full attention of the Indians. Their lead-off batter's eyes widened and he stepped out and looked at his dugout, as if to say, *Wow. Could be a long night, boys.*

Zoom's next pitch was high before he blew the kid away with two more fastballs, the last one catching the outside corner. It was an impossible pitch to hit, even if you could catch up to it, which the kid couldn't.

As the batter trudged back to the dugout muttering to himself, the rest of the Orioles seemed to breathe a sigh of relief.

Their ace was back. And throwing serious heat.

No, it didn't guarantee a win. No one was dumb enough

to think that. But at least the O's had their best pitcher going for them and the kid seemed to be in a good frame of mind, which was all you could ask for in a big game like this.

Zoom got the next batter on a weak ground ball to second that Justin gobbled up easily. Now Mickey began to settle down, too. It felt good to be calling pitches again, trying to outthink the hitters, especially when a pitcher seemed locked in early, as Zoom did now.

It wasn't rocket science, what they were doing with the signs. One finger for a fastball; two for a curve; three for a changeup. Pretty standard stuff. But since Zoom could throw all three pitches well, it was fun trying to mix things up and keep the hitters off balance.

Especially since, if he fell behind in the count with a breaking ball or changeup, Zoom could always come back with his money pitch: the blazing fastball. Which he could seemingly throw over the plate whenever he wanted to.

Zoom got the next batter on a 3-and-2 curveball to end the inning and quietly pumped his fist. Mickey watched him jog off the field. There was something else totally different about the boy now, something Mickey couldn't quite figure out.

Then it hit him: Zoom was smiling!

Mickey wondered if it was the first time he'd ever seen him smile during a game. He'd seen Zoom flash a cruel version of a smile off the field, like when he'd jabbed a finger in Mickey's gut and suggested he lay off the snowballs and eat more salad.

Yeah, like *that* would ever happen. Mickey chuckled.

Or like he'd give up wings at Augie's just to look sleek in his uniform. But it was definitely great to see Zoom finally having fun playing ball.

As soon as Mickey reached the dugout, Hunter greeted him.

"We're going to win this thing," he said emphatically. "You can take that to the bank."

Mickey was astonished. "We haven't even batted yet. And you, Mr. Gloom and Doom, Dr. Depresso, are guaranteeing victory? Did you forget who's throwing for them?"

They looked out at the mound, where a lanky blond-haired kid who seemed to be all arms and legs was warming up.

"Chris Jor-gen-son," Mickey said, drawing out each syllable for maximum effect. "Do I need to remind you that next to Zoom, he's the fastest pitcher in the league?"

"Still," Hunter said, "our guy's looking strong, dude. And check this out."

He jerked his head in Zoom's direction. Instead of sitting sullenly at the end of the bench with his arms crossed, the way he usually did, Zoom was standing on the top step of the dugout with Corey, Evan, and Justin, all of them talking animatedly.

"We're one big happy family!" Hunter said, grinning. "Talent, toughness, and togetherness—you can't beat a team with those ingredients!"

"Thank you, Coach Bill Belichick," Mickey said. "I just hope you're right."

The game was still scoreless in the bottom of the fifth inning, with Zoom and Chris Jorgenson locked in a classic pitchers' duel. Their stat lines were remarkably similar: Zoom had walked two and given up one hit. Chris had given up two walks and two hits.

This being the championship game, the teams could use their best pitchers for all six innings of regulation play. If the game went extra innings, though, both would have to be relieved.

Everyone knew time was running out. The tension was definitely rising.

"We need to score *now*!" Katelyn shouted as the O's came off the field.

"Tell that to him," Hunter muttered, pointing to the Indians pitcher taking his warm-up tosses.

"Oh, what happened to Mr. I-Guarantee-a-Win?" Mickey asked. "Mr. Talent-Toughness-and-Togetherness?"

Hunter shook his head. "Didn't know their guy was gonna turn into Justin Verlander."

Katelyn stomped over to Hunter and got in his face.

"He's *not* Justin Verlander, nerd," she said evenly. "He's just a skinny kid who was in my art class last year."

"If he paints like he pitches," Hunter said, "he must be a freakin' Picasso."

"That did it, nerd!" Katelyn roared. "I've *had* it with your negative crap!"

She cocked her fist and advanced on Hunter, who grabbed his batting helmet and fled to the on-deck circle as the rest of the Orioles laughed.

"You *better* get on base, nerd," she hissed. "Because you know what I'll do to you if you don't."

What happened next left Mickey and the rest of the Orioles shaking their heads in amazement.

Hunter had one of his best at-bats all season. He was up there swinging, but he was patient, too, looking for his pitch. And when Chris Jorgenson missed high with a 3–2 fastball, Hunter tossed his bat aside and scampered down to first base with a grateful look.

"Fear of a beatdown—the ultimate motivator," Gabe said with a smile.

Mickey nodded. "Always is. Did you see how focused he was? If he struck out, he would've had to run straight to the parking lot and wait for his mommy."

The walk seemed to rattle Chris. He managed to get Katelyn on a slow roller to first. But after getting two strikes on Sammy, he threw four straight pitches up and out of the strike zone to give the Orioles runners on first and second with one out.

Mickey was up. As he was leaving the on-deck circle, he felt a hand on his shoulder.

"I know, Dad," he said. "Pick out something I can hit hard, right?"

But when he turned around, it was Zoom.

"Their pitcher's leaving everything up," he said. "Which means he's not following through. Which means he's tired. If you like letter-high fastballs, this could be like Christmas morning."

Unbelievable, Mickey thought. A week ago, the kid was a silent, sulking cancer on the team. Now he looked like he wanted to win more than anyone else out there.

Mickey flashed him a thumbs-up.

Zoom's read of the situation proved to be dead-on. Chris was struggling to keep the ball down. His first two pitches were up and away, not even close to being strikes. He kicked the rosin bag in frustration as the Indians coach implored him to "Bring it down a little!"

Yeah, do that, Mickey thought. Be a good kid and listen to your coach.

Chris's next pitch was a shoulder-high fastball. In retrospect, Mickey's dad would have yelled at him to lay off, to wait for something in the strike zone. But Mickey's eyes lit up and he swung.

Instantly he realized he was late on the pitch. And what he hit wasn't a sharp line drive in the gap, but a little flare over the second baseman's head. It wouldn't have made anyone's highlight reel, unless they had a highlight reel for Worst Swings/Good Results.

But there it was, dropping softly in front of the hard-charging center fielder for a base hit. And here was Hunter rounding third and dashing home with the Orioles' biggest run of the season.

O's 1, Indians 0.

As he touched the plate, Hunter shot a triumphant look at Katelyn. Even standing on first base, Mickey could read his lips as he taunted her in a singsong voice: *"You can't kill me now, you can't kill me now . . ."*

Chris bore down after that and struck out Corey and Spencer to end the inning. But the damage was done. The Indians jogged off the field with their heads down.

The Orioles, on the other hand, were jacked. They were three outs away from the championship.

As Zoom raced out to the mound, Mickey turned and delivered a warning to the rest of the O's taking the field:

"Don't even *think* of a team meeting on the mound. If any of you say anything stupid to my pitcher to mess up his concentration, I will personally kick you in the butt."

Mickey caught himself.

Had he really just said that? *My* pitcher? Wow, what a difference one game made.

But Mickey proved to be right: Zoom didn't need anyone offering advice or telling him to relax or spouting any of the other meaningless baseball clichés kids rattle off when the game was on the line. His face was a grim mask and he went right after the Indians, throwing even harder now.

He struck out the first batter on four pitches, the last one a curveball that seemed to break from somewhere near the Indians dugout. The next batter hit a comebacker to the mound that Zoom pounced on for the second out.

Now, with the Orioles on their toes and holding their breath behind him, he got ahead of the third batter with two fastballs that split the middle of the plate. Beautiful, Mickey thought. He put down three fingers. Throw this kid a changeup now and he'll practically screw himself into the ground thinking it's a fastball.

Zoom nodded at the sign, went into his windup, and delivered. It was a terrific changeup, with the Indians batter starting his swing before the ball was halfway to the plate. But somehow the kid managed an excuse-me swing and lifted a pop-up to Hunter in foul territory.

When the little third baseman squeezed the ball in his glove, Zoom whooped and shot his arms to the sky in celebration as the Orioles raced to the mound and buried him in a big, sloppy pig-pile.

As soon they finally untangled themselves, Katelyn punched a fist in the air and cried, "YES! Now we get the Huntington Yankees! Oh, would I love to beat their butts! You have no idea!"

Sammy nodded. "You probably don't know about them, Z," he said. "But they're, like, the best team in the area. Not to mention the most arrogant jerks around."

Just like that, Zoom's smile vanished, replaced by a pained expression.

"Oh, I know all about them," he said softly. "That's my old team."

24

Zoom's bombshell announcement left the Orioles speechless.

They stared slack-jawed at their pitcher for what seemed like an eternity. Finally Mickey's dad cleared his throat.

"Well . . ." he said. Then, after a long pause: "We should, um, probably discuss this further, shouldn't we? Okay, the snowballs are on me. Anyone who wants to stay is welcome to join us."

Many of the Orioles had to leave to catch rides with their parents. But Mickey and his dad, along with Zoom, Gabe, Sammy, and Katelyn, walked over to Abby's stand.

Abby scurried around filling orders, once again calling out Mickey for his usual boring request. ("Your attention, please, ladies and gentlemen! For the four hundred and seventy-eighth day in a row, daring young Michael J. Labriolga has ordered—ta-da!—another grape snowball!")

After everyone was served, she joined them at the big picnic table out front while they slurped their icy treats and listened to Zoom with rapt attention.

"Not a fun team to play for, the Yankees," he was saying.

He reached into his equipment bag and pulled out his cell phone.

"Here, look at this," he said.

The screen filled with a team photo of a dozen boys in gleaming white uniforms with pinstripes and navy HY caps standing stiffly behind a huge banner proclaiming:

HUNTINGTON YANKEES:
UNMATCHED EXCELLENCE IN YOUTH BASEBALL

There, in the middle, stood their coach, the infamous Al "Money" Mayhew. He was wearing his own pristine Yankees uni, the jersey fitting snugly over his prodigious gut, and he had a smug smile plastered on his jowly features.

"Bottom row, second from the right, if you're trying to find me," Zoom said, holding the phone up for everyone to see. He shook his head ruefully. "Does it seem like I'm having a great time?"

Mickey studied the picture. Zoom's face looked as if it might crack into a dozen pieces. It was a classic example of a kid straining to smile when he didn't feel like it, except he had to because some hypercheerful adult was pointing a camera and making goofy faces and imploring everyone to say "Cheese!"

The result for Zoom was more of a grimace than a smile, like someone who was experiencing severe gas pains and would be hustling off to the bathroom as soon as the stupid picture was taken.

Mickey had seen that look before, in the photos of Zoom on the Elite Arms Web site.

"So, if you want the whole story," Zoom said, "the Yankees recruited me. And I really wanted to play for them. We had just moved to Huntington and everyone said they were the best team around.

"And they *were* the best. They played on the best fields, had the best equipment—three-hundred-dollar bats, two-hundred-and-fifty-dollar gloves, brand-new batting gloves for every game. Most of the kids were rich; only a few of us weren't. And we never felt like we really fit in."

He chuckled weakly at the memory.

"If I'd ever asked my dad for a three-hundred-dollar bat, he would've looked at me like I was crazy."

The rest of the Orioles nodded in agreement.

"But what was *really* different," Zoom continued, "was all the trash-talking they did. Practices, games, it didn't matter. They went around acting like they were the greatest players in the whole world. And they made fun of everyone else—how they played, how they looked, whatever. And Coach Mayhew loved it! He told the parents all the trash talk showed we had a lot of fight in us, and that our confidence was sky-high."

Mickey glanced at his dad, who was shaking his head and frowning.

"So I started acting like the other kids," Zoom went on. "I thought that was what Coach wanted and my teammates expected. We had a great season and won the regional, and I pitched pretty well . . ."

He looked away before saying softly, "But my dad didn't like what was happening to me. Then we moved here, and I started playing for you guys."

At this, Katelyn put down her snowball and glared at Zoom.

"Well, I agree with your dad," she said. "During practice, you acted like you were the best pitcher in the world and you were single-handedly going to win the championship for us. You insisted we call you by that stupid nickname. Then you showed up for the first game with your nerd entourage. What was up with *that*?"

Mickey winced. Oh, boy, he thought. As usual, Katelyn was as subtle as a punch to the jaw.

Zoom's face reddened.

"I know, I know," he said. "Those were just three kids from the neighborhood. They weren't really my posse or anything. They were just, like, bored. So they started hanging around me and coming to the games."

Katelyn rolled her eyes and muttered, "Three of the lamest losers *ever*. In the entire history of baseball, there's never been—"

Mickey's dad held up his hands. "Maybe we don't need to get into that right now . . ."

"No, it's okay," Zoom said. "They *were* lame. And I was in full butthead mode. You were right to call me on it, Coach. When you benched me, I was so mad I thought about quitting. Even told my dad I was done playing for you guys."

"That would have been a huge mistake," said Gabe. "And a huge loss for the team."

Typical Gabe, Mickey thought with admiration. Supporting the guy who had taken his position.

"That's what a friend kept telling me," Zoom said, and he looked meaningfully at Abby.

"Yeah, you're a star," said Abby, making Mickey's stomach turn. "Even if you are obnoxious."

Okay, that was better.

Zoom actually laughed. Then he went on: "I love baseball too much to quit. But there's more to it than that."

He turned to Sammy. "You guys know how to have fun out there"—here he looked at Mickey—"even while you take the game seriously. That's a big difference between this team and the Yankees."

Mickey felt a rush of pride. "I wouldn't want it any other way," he said.

Zoom nodded. "Right. But it was an adjustment for me. I realized I'd have to change if I wanted to keep playing. At least if I wanted to keep playing for the Orioles. Which I do."

Mickey's dad said, "That's kind of what we were all hoping for, Z. In the back of my mind, I thought: Any kid that jumps in and saves a lady choking in a restaurant—yeah, I saw the article in the paper—is a kid I want on my team."

"The Heimlich Hero!" Sammy cried.

"Clutch on the mound—and in a medical emergency!" Gabe added.

Zoom groaned good-naturedly and Mickey gave him a fist bump. For a moment, no one spoke. Then Katelyn stood and stared at Zoom, and shook her head.

"Is this where we're all supposed to applaud because you're having a major attitude shift—even though it's about a month too late—and everyone's saying nice things about you and you promise you're not going to be a selfish brat anymore, and blah, blah, blah?"

"Katelyn, please . . ." Mickey's dad said.

"Because I really don't care about any of that," she continued heatedly. "All I care about is that you're ready to back up all your big talk and pitch lights-out against the Yankees. This is a huge game for us, okay? Do you get that? So whatever you do, don't blow it."

Way to dial down the pressure, Mickey thought. But Zoom seemed unfazed as he locked eyes with Katelyn, neither one blinking.

"I'll be ready," he said evenly.

"You *better* be, nerd," Katelyn said.

Mickey's dad rose to his feet.

"Well," he said, "on that happy note, I guess we can bring this meeting to a close. We'll have a practice before the Yankees game. I'll e-mail everyone the details."

Then a big smile creased his face.

"Oh, and uh, Zoom?" he continued. "There *is* something else you can do for us. Besides pitch well next week."

"What's that, Coach?" Zoom asked.

"Two words: *scouting report*. There are probably some kids on this Yankees team that you played with last season, right? Which means you know what their pitchers throw, what their hitters like to hit, which of their kids are a threat to steal, etc. That kind of information could be very helpful."

Now Zoom was smiling, too.

"Yeah," he said. "I could definitely do that."

He looked at the team photo on his cell again and nodded.

"In fact," he said, "it would be my pleasure."

Mickey heard the doorbell and the fierce knocking that followed and thought, I could just ignore it.

It's early, right? I could just sit here in my pajamas and keep watching TV and pretend not to hear anything. Maybe she'll go away. Yeah, that's it. Maybe she'll think I'm sick or dead and just go away.

But he knew better.

Neither sickness nor death would stop her. No, you could have the worst disease in the whole world or be a withered corpse already and she'd still get in your face if there was something on her mind.

He peered out the window and sighed. It was Katelyn, all right. This time she appeared to be carrying an iPad in one hand. The other hand was pounding on the door so hard it was rattling the hinges.

When Mickey finally answered it, she blew past him into the living room.

"Something wrong with your hearing, nerd?" she asked. "I've been out there for, like, ages."

Then she whipped around and gaped at him.

"Are those . . . *pajamas*?" she asked. "Really, dude? You look like a walking tablecloth. Or a beach umbrella with legs."

"Good morning to you, too, Katelyn," Mickey said. "Anyone ever tell you you're like a little ray of sunshine?"

She ignored him and plunked herself down in front of the coffee table. Then she turned on her iPad.

"Oh, it's starting already!" she said gleefully. "Wait till you see the crap they're posting. These little weasels are unbelievable."

Mickey rubbed the sleep from his eyes.

"Okay, when you say 'these little weasels,'" he began, "you mean . . ."

She looked at him as if he'd just shot to number one on the World's Dumbest Kid list.

"The Huntington Yankees, nerd!" she said. "Duh-h-h! Who else would I be talking about? The game's not till next week and they're killing us already!"

"Killing us . . . how?" Mickey asked.

"On their stupid Web site!" Katelyn said. "I know, I know . . . you're shocked to hear they have a Web site. I was, too."

She turned the screen so Mickey could see. There, at the top of the Yankees' home page was the headline FIFTEEN YEARS OF YOUTH BASEBALL EXCELLENCE.

Directly underneath was a large photo of Al "Money" Mayhew addressing his team and a small knot of parents, who appeared to be hanging on his every word.

"Don't you just love that slick grin of his?" Katelyn said. "You know the minute he left those folks he was looking around for a dog to kick."

To the right of the photo was a blog post titled YANKEES HEAVY FAVORITES TO TURN BACK DULANEY ORIOLES.

Mickey began to read aloud:

"'Veteran Yankees coach Al "Money" Mayhew said he anticipates few problems when the Yankees take on the Dulaney Orioles in the new one-game regional final to be played at Huntington's Carter Field next weekend.

"'"My team is as ready as it'll ever be," Mayhew said. "We've posted another excellent season, as expected. But to be honest, I don't know much at all about the Orioles."'"

Katelyn snorted. "Of *course* he doesn't know much about us—because we're too trivial for the mighty Yankees to worry about! Too beneath them! Why study up on the other team when you're just going to squash 'em like a bug anyway?"

She jumped up and began pacing about the room. As Mickey watched her, he had to suppress a grin. Mount St. Katelyn was ready to erupt and he had a front-row seat to the gathering firestorm.

"Can you imagine any other coach saying that?" Katelyn continued, her voice rising. "Huh? Can you imagine any other coach being so disrespectful of an opponent? Who does he think he is? Like he's God's gift to baseball or something!

"And who made the Yankees the heavy favorites? ESPN? Yahoo Sports? The *Baltimore Sun*? Or just a big, fat blowhard named Al Mayhew?"

She stopped and sank back in the chair, glowering.

"Are you through?" Mickey asked. "Can I continue reading now?"

She waved her hand and muttered, "By all means. Be my guest."

Mickey read: "'"Nevertheless, we're confident in our own abilities," Mayhew added. "As I told our team at practice the other day, we really haven't been challenged this season. Not many teams in the state play at our level of competition, of course, so that's part of it. We've played some games that we won so easily that, frankly, our kids didn't even get their uniforms dirty. But I'm sure the Orioles are a perfectly fine team. And we're looking forward to any challenge they can present."'"

Katelyn shot to her feet again.

"So-o-o condescending! 'Any challenge they can present!' You see what he's doing there? It's like he's patting us on the head! 'Oh, you're a perfectly fine little team, but we're only playing you because we have to. And we certainly don't expect to even break a sweat! So be good little boys and girls and take your fifteen–two beatdown or whatever it is we decide to give you. And don't give us a hard time, you hear?'"

She shook her head in amazement. "Does that make you want to barf or what?"

Mickey nodded.

The Yankees' arrogance *was* unbelievable. And it never seemed to end. He'd been hearing tales about Money Mayhew and his egotistical players ever since he was a little kid, when the older boys in town talked about what a circus it was to face the Yankees.

Between the trash-talking from the players and all the

sneaky things their coach did to rattle the other team—like loudly calling a time-out just when the opposing pitcher went into his windup, or yelling "OH, YEAH!" every time the ump called a strike on an opposing batter—a game against the Yankees felt like a combination of a schoolyard brawl and a psychological test.

So Mickey wasn't exactly shocked that there was smack talk on the Yankees' Web site a week before the showdown with the Orioles. No, he would have been more shocked if there *wasn't*.

"But you can't get caught up in all that, Katelyn," he said. "Let them talk all they want. Just ignore them. Don't fire back. No posts, no e-mails, no tweets. There are other things you can do that would help us way more."

"Oh, yeah?" she said. "Like what?"

"Like go easy on Zoom, for starters," Mickey said.

Katelyn's eyes narrowed. "Oh, that was too much for you the other night, nerd? Him finally being called out for being an egotistical pain in the butt, with his show-off plays, dumb little posse, and everything else?"

"He's trying to be a better teammate—anyone can see that," Mickey said. "Give him a chance. And what was that you-*better*-be-ready-for-the-Yankees stuff?"

Katelyn sneered. "Was I being too hard on your boy? Oh, I'm *so-o-o* sorry!"

"I just don't see how threatening a kid helps him pitch better," Mickey said.

"I didn't *threaten* him," Katelyn said. "I didn't say I was gonna hunt him down if he blows it."

"Yeah, you sort of did," Mickey said. "The point is, we need everyone working together to have any shot of beating that team."

Katelyn stared at him for a few seconds. Finally she sighed and looked longingly at her iPad.

"How 'bout we post just one little comment? Tell 'em they're big, fat losers and we can't wait to crush them and their smug, dog-breath coach?" she asked.

"Wouldn't that sort of contradict the just-ignore-them strategy?" Mickey said.

Katelyn stomped her foot in frustration. She scooped up her iPad and headed for the door.

"Fine," she snarled. "We'll do it your way, nerd. Peace and love and all that crap—until we beat their brains in next week."

Well, that's one way of putting it, Mickey thought as he heard the door slam behind him.

The practice before the Yankees game was the best one of the season, in Mickey's opinion. Everywhere you looked, the Orioles were smiling as they went about their work. Even his dad seemed to be having a great time as he put them through drills and talked strategy.

They were having so much fun that, during breaks, no one wanted to leave the field, even to get a drink of water. Instead, they gathered together to hold goofy competitions, like who could make the best behind-the-back catch of a fly ball and who could run the bases backward the fastest.

"Watch this!" Sammy yelled at one point. He stood ten feet from the outfield fence and nodded at Ethan. "Let it fly, E."

Ethan wound up and threw a soft, arcing pop-up that seemed headed for the scoreboard beyond center field.

But Sammy raced back, hurdled the fence, and made a jaw-dropping backhand catch in midair before crashing to the ground on the other side. He rolled over twice and shot his glove into the air so everyone could see the ball peeking out from the webbing.

"And the judges give that a score of—oh, my, I can't believe it!—nine-point-nine-eight!" Gabe gushed in the awestruck tones of an Olympics announcer. "That was an incredible catch! But apparently there was a slight deduction on style points. These judges are tough today, folks, I'll tell you that!"

"Yeah, and they're also blind!" Sammy bellowed in mock outrage, brushing the dirt from his jersey. "That was a ten all the way! Are you kidding? That had *SportsCenter* highlight written all over it!"

Zoom hummed the famous *SportsCenter* jingle. "Da, da, da, DA, DA, DA!"

"In fact, I just changed my mind!" Sammy went on. "Forget *SportsCenter*. It was one of the finest catches in baseball history!"

As the rest of the Orioles cracked up, Katelyn put her hands on her hips and said, "You *do* realize, nerd, that the game's been around for, like, one hundred and fifty years? So you're saying that was one of the top catches in all that time?"

"Absolutely," Sammy said. "The sheer athleticism, the pinpoint timing, the poetry of the leap . . ."

"'The poetry of the leap'?" Hunter said. "Seriously, dude? 'Poetry'?"

Which only sent Sammy on another sputtering rant about how genuine baseball talent was undervalued these days and had been for years—well, at least since he was ten years old.

Mickey was loving every minute of it.

The Orioles were totally focused—this was the sharpest

they'd looked in infield and outfield practice in a long time. And yet they were totally loose, too, which was so important going into a big game like this.

The way Mickey saw it, all the pressure was on the Yankees. They were the hotshot team with the monster rep and the rich legacy, expected to steamroll the poor little outgunned Orioles.

If the Orioles somehow found a way to win, it would be the biggest upset in local youth baseball in years.

They'd have to throw a parade for us, Mickey thought. On the other hand, Huntington would be plunged into mourning. The town hall would be decorated with black bunting and folks would be wailing in the streets. Meanwhile the Yankees themselves would be so devastated and ashamed by the loss they'd probably wear paper bags over their heads for months.

The Orioles were just as energized during batting practice as they had been in the drills.

According to Zoom, Kevin Milo was likely to be the Yankees starter. He was a big, hard-throwing right hander, so Coach humped up on his BP fastball to get the Orioles used to the pitching speed they'd be seeing Friday night.

Hunter was the first batter. A few of the Orioles, Mickey included, whistled admiringly as they watched Coach's first pitches to the little third baseman.

Hunter himself stepped out and said, "Dang, you still got it, Coach! If that Kevin Milo kid throws as hard, I just hope he has good control!"

"Don't be nervous, Hunter," Gabe called. "Even if the kid's a little wild, what's the worst that could happen?"

"How about Hunter gets beaned and starts flopping on the ground like a fish?" Katelyn offered helpfully.

"Or he takes a fastball in the ribs and can't breathe or bend over for a couple of days?" Sammy said.

"Or Milo drills him in the leg and he's wearing a cast and on crutches for the rest of the summer?" Corey added.

Hunter turned pale and stepped out again.

"Uh, guys, maybe we could do without all the graphic scenarios," Coach said. "Do we really think that's helpful?"

"Okay, maybe not," Katelyn said, giggling. "Hey, Hunter, just ignore everything we said."

Even with Coach throwing hard, most of the Orioles were getting around on his pitches and driving the ball. Mickey was one of the last to hit. When he finally stepped in, his dad threw him a fastball that crashed into the backstop and seemed to be the hardest pitch of the afternoon.

"Shouldn't you be getting tired?" Mickey yelled playfully. "A seventy-year-old man still throwing that hard? Your arm's gonna fall off!"

His dad grunted. "Don't worry about me, kid. Just worry about getting that bat going early when you face Milo Friday night."

Toward the end of practice, Mickey's dad called the team together. The Orioles sprawled in the grass along the third-base line. They were tired but exhilarated by how sharp they had looked and how much fun they'd just had.

"All right," Coach said, "to close things out today, we have a special guest speaker. And this speaker is—drum roll, please!—Zoom.

"He's already given us a pretty good scouting report on

the Yankees—at least on the kids he played with last season who are still on this year's team. But he brought up a few other interesting points, which I've asked him to pass along to you guys. Zoom?"

Zoom stood and nervously surveyed his teammates.

"Um, what I told Coach is that playing the Yankees will be totally different from any other team you've ever played," he began. "And the main thing we all have to do is remain calm. Which isn't easy when you play those guys. Especially down there.

"Carter Field is like a miniversion of, like, a college stadium. And the Yankees have a lot of fans. And they're *loud*. The whole atmosphere is intimidating. I've seen visiting teams come in there and turn white when they see the packed stands and hear the crowd roar for the first time.

"Another thing to watch out for," Zoom continued, "is Moose Mayhew."

This set off a chorus of boos.

"You mean *Marvin*?" Katelyn said.

Zoom grinned. He appeared to be settling down now.

"He's an okay defensive catcher," continued Zoom. "Although, in my opinion, Mickey's much better all-around. With a way better arm."

Mickey shot to his feet and bowed deeply as the Orioles chuckled.

"Mickey's way nicer, too," Zoom said, grinning.

"Awww!" went the rest of the Orioles.

"You two wanna hug it out?" Ethan asked.

Zoom's face turned red, but he pressed on.

"Okay, okay. But what Moose can *really* do behind the

plate is talk. In fact, he won't shut up the entire time you're up at bat. You have to be ready for that. He'll start in before the first pitch, with stuff like: 'You can't hit my pitcher. Do you know who that is? Do you have any idea? That's Kevin Milo, the strikeout king! He's gonna ring you up on three pitches! Four, tops. You have no shot against him.'"

"Sounds like a major dork," Sammy said to more chuckles.

Zoom nodded. "Yep, he is. Sometimes the umpire will tell him to shut up when he starts the trash-talking. But I wouldn't count on it Friday night. Not with the game at their home field. The umpires let them get away with practically everything there. So Moose will just keep yapping. And if he thinks it's starting to get to you, he'll yap even more. You can count on that."

Zoom paused. "Which brings us to his dad, Money Mayhew."

This elicited a fresh round of boos, mixed with hisses.

"You've all heard about him. And whatever you've heard is probably not an exaggeration. He won't shut up all game long, either."

"Okay, now we know why the kid's a dork," Sammy said.

"It's in his DNA," Katelyn said. She turned to Hunter. "And before you ask what DNA is, nerd, it's—"

"Please," Coach said. "Can we just let Zoom finish? Hunter, look it up when you get home."

Zoom waited for the laughter to die down. "Moose's dad will say anything to disrupt the other team's concentration. He'll yell at the other team's batter, 'This kid can't hit!'

Or he'll yell to his pitcher, 'He keeps crowding the plate like that, stick one in his ear!'"

"Great," Hunter moaned. "And I was just starting to relax . . ."

"Or else he'll dog the other team's pitcher," Zoom continued. "He'll keep up a steady commentary about how nervous the pitcher is, or how wild he looks, or how he's starting to get tired. Anything to get the kid rattled."

He shook his head in wonder. "Can you believe he used to make us call him Coach Money?"

"Seriously?" Corey said.

Zoom nodded. "Oh, yeah. He made me run laps once 'cause I just called him 'Coach.'"

"Oh . . . my . . . God!" Katelyn said.

"Anyway, that's all I got," Zoom said. He started to sit, then said, "Except . . . I would *love* to beat those guys. I really would."

When Zoom was finished, no one spoke for a moment.

Then Coach said, "So there it is. The keys to playing well Friday night: tune out the atmosphere and the trash-talking; play your game. Easier said than done, I know. But I have faith in this team. You're going to do fine. Any questions before we call it a day?"

Hunter raised his hand.

"I think I got it," he said. "Is DNA a rapper?"

As the Orioles exploded in guffaws, Coach smiled and shook his head.

"Wonder if Money Mayhew's ever been asked that," he said. "I'm gonna go out on a limb here and say no."

The mall was busy for a hot Thursday night in July. Mickey, Abby, and Gabe had just rounded a corner on the second level when Mickey stopped suddenly. He opened his arms wide and smiled.

"Ahhh, here it is!" he said. "The most wonderful place on earth!"

Abby and Gabe looked at each other.

"The *food court*?" Abby said. "*That's* the most wonderful place on earth?"

Mickey nodded. He inhaled deeply, a blissful look on his face.

"Smell that?" he said. "Oh, that's wonderful! That's why we're here."

"I thought we were here for batting gloves," Gabe said.

"Shhhh," Mickey said, gazing lovingly at the bustling scene in front of him. "Please. Don't ruin the moment."

His dad had dropped the three of them off a few minutes earlier. Twenty-four hours before the Orioles' showdown with the Huntington Yankees, Mickey had been too amped up to hang around the house. So he'd called Gabe and Abby and proposed a short road trip, which both had been up for immediately.

Mickey stared wide-eyed into a vast, teeming, neon-lit slice of heaven that offered every kind of delectable food imaginable: burgers, fries, pizza, subs, sushi, Mexican food, Asian food, smoothies, pretzels, brownies, cookies, ice cream, and much more.

The smells wafting from all directions made him half mad with longing.

Without taking his eyes from the scene, he said, "Yes, we're here for batting gloves. But we have to be at our physical and mental peak tomorrow. So we're here to carbo-load for the big game with the Yankees, too. Right, Gabe?"

"Yeah, right," Gabe said. "Who are you kidding? You'd carbo-load for a game of Scrabble."

"I can't argue with that," Mickey said. "Well, I *could*. But that would make me a liar."

"You know, lots of runners don't even carbo-load anymore," Abby said. "I just read that. Many endurance athletes now believe it doesn't do any good."

"Well, baseball players still believe in it," Mickey said. "At least *this* one does. Let's eat."

The dizzying array of choices paralyzed Mickey with indecision, as usual. Abby quickly chose a grilled chicken sandwich and Gabe bought a slice of pizza and a soda. But it took Mickey a full ten minutes of wandering hungrily from vendor to vendor before he finally settled on a burrito stuffed with rice, beans, chicken, guacamole, corn, sour cream, and green chili sauce.

They found a table on the outskirts of the octagonal-shaped room and dug into their food.

"Are you getting nervous yet?" Abby asked. "With the big game so close?"

"No," Mickey said. "Can't wait, really."

"Seriously?" she said. "The thought of playing in front of all those people, that doesn't make you nervous?"

"I'm okay so far," he said, taking another monster bite of his food.

"All those Yankees fans pressing in all around you, the haters heckling you and clutching their throats and screaming that you're going to choke—that won't bother you?"

"Well . . ." Mickey said.

"Plus having to face a big-time baseball superpower under the direction of a maniac coach and his possibly demented offspring, both of whom will stop at nothing to win—you're ready for all that?"

Mickey put down his burrito and threw his hands up in exasperation.

"Okay, congratulations," he said. "Now you're officially freaking me out."

"Good," Abby said as she and Gabe cracked up. "I was beginning to think you were a robot or something. But, hey, no worries. I'm sure you'll do fine."

"Thanks for the vote of confidence," Mickey said glumly. Then he looked down at his food and brightened. "Anyway, nothing you say is gonna spoil my appetite for this baby."

"That's, like, the biggest burrito I've ever seen," Abby said.

"It's the size of a shoe box!" Gabe said.

Mickey took another bite and nodded contentedly. "Go big or go home—that's always been my motto."

"It's such a gloppy mess," Abby said. "Is there *anything* they didn't put on that? I'm surprised it doesn't have, like, Reese's Pieces."

"Not a bad idea," Mickey said. "I'll suggest that to the Best Burrito management before we leave. But, honestly? It really *is* the best burrito I've ever had."

A few minutes later, Mickey noticed two little kids at the next table staring at him and whispering to each other. They were maybe seven and nine years old, sitting on the other side of their parents, who were chatting away, oblivious to what their boys were doing.

"Why are those kids looking at you?" Abby asked.

Mickey shrugged. "Probably the usual reasons. They recognize superior brainpower and athletic ability when they see it."

Abby looked at the burrito and wrinkled her nose. "Or maybe they can't believe anyone would eat anything that gross."

"Sure," Mickey said. "It could be that, too."

A moment later, the two little kids stood and approached their table.

"Incoming," Mickey whispered. "Brace yourself. They probably want my autograph. This could get awkward for you guys."

When he looked up, the two boys were standing in front of him.

"Our big brother plays for the Huntington Yankees," the older one said, scowling.

"Yeah," the younger one said.

"And they're gonna kick your butt," the older one said.

"Yeah," the younger one said.

"Our dad says they're gonna beat you like a rented mule," the older one said.

"Yeah," the younger one said.

With that, the two turned and went back to their seats.

"What charming children," Abby said.

"If the little kids are like that," Gabe said, "imagine what the rest of the Yankees crowd will be like tomorrow night."

Abby nodded. "They'll probably be waving pitchforks and carrying torches by the time you guys show up."

Mickey was so stunned he sat there slack-jawed, holding the burrito in front of his lips.

"Now he looks like the Burrito Whisperer," Gabe said. He tapped Mickey on the shoulder. "Hey, you okay?"

"How . . . did they know I play for the Orioles?" Mickey asked finally.

Abby and Gabe looked at each other and chuckled.

"Well, Detective Labriogla," Gabe said, "I think they pretty much figured it out by looking at your shirt."

Mickey looked down and realized he was wearing his black Dulaney Orioles team jersey from last season.

"Okay," he said sheepishly, "that was *really* dumb. Can we keep that to ourselves? It'll be our little secret, okay?"

Gabe shrugged. "What happens in the food court stays in the food court. Everyone knows that."

Mickey smiled gratefully. Then he pushed his tray aside and stood.

"If you guys are through, let's go buy some batting gloves," he said.

Abby pointed to the half of the burrito still on his plate.

"What about the world's best burrito?" she said. "You're not gonna finish it?"

"No, those little brats ruined my appetite," Mickey said. "Besides, the whole carbo-loading thing is probably a myth, anyway."

The Orioles were dazzled. They stood at the entrance of Carter Field with their gear bags slung around their shoulders, gaping at the most gorgeous little ballpark any of them had ever seen.

If this isn't baseball heaven, Mickey thought, it's in the same area code.

The outfield and infield grass was greener than the felt on any pool table. It looked spray-painted and was mowed in elegant, precise diamond patterns, just like in a major-league stadium.

The red-brown dirt of the basepaths had been painstakingly raked until it seemed not even one errant pebble remained. The gleaming white bases and the freshly limed foul lines and batter's box seemed to shimmer in the last rays of the evening sun.

"I'd be afraid to spit a sunflower seed in here," Sammy said in a hushed voice. "They'd probably have me arrested."

"Plus they'd make you vacuum it up before they threw you in the slammer," Zoom said. "Believe me, I know."

The rest of the ballpark was equally charming and picturesque.

Beyond the center-field wall was a big digital scoreboard with HUNTINGTON YANKEES spelled out in big, block letters and VISITORS below that. On an elevated slope to the right was a giant display of red, white, and pink flowers bordered by newly painted white stones. Behind it stood two towering flagpoles, with the American and Maryland-state flags rippling majestically in the breeze.

"The place is almost too nice to play in," Hunter said. "Feels like we should just take a picture of it and go home."

"We're not going anywhere, nerd," Katelyn growled. "No, we're here for *them*."

She pointed across the field to where the Yankees were stretching and loosening their arms to rock music blaring over the sound system. They were wearing crisp, bright white pants—the whitest the Orioles had ever seen—and jerseys with classic navy-blue pinstripes.

"I don't see a single wrinkle on those unis," Corey marveled.

"Or any grass stains, or even a speck of dirt," Ethan said. "It's like they just stepped out of Bubble Wrap or something."

Zoom chuckled. "Yeah, forgot to tell you about that. Coach Mayhew used to yell at us if we got our uniforms dirty before games."

The Yankees' navy caps appeared to be brand-new, as if the price tags had been removed seconds earlier. Even their black spikes looked freshly polished.

It was all too much for Katelyn to handle.

After taking a quick glance around to make sure Coach wasn't in the vicinity, she shouted, "Hey, nerds, do your mommies iron your nice little unis? And dress you before every game?"

Only one of the Yankees seemed to have heard her. He whipped his head around and stared at her for several seconds, chomping thoughtfully on his gum, as if trying to assess whether this piddling little insult was worth a response.

Finally he blew a big bubble, smiled, and turned away.

The message was clear: *Whoever you are, angry girl, don't think your petty gibes can get under the skin of the mighty Yankees.*

Which only made Katelyn even more incensed.

"God, I hope that little nerd plays the infield and I have to slide into him," she hissed. "Because I swear I'll kick him right in the—"

"Uh, uh, uh! Don't say it!" Mickey said. "This is no time to go all potty mouth. Let's get a good warm-up and concentrate on the game, okay?"

Katelyn scowled and scuffed the dirt with her toe in frustration.

"The voice of reason," she said sullenly. "Anyone ever tell you you're like a twelve-year-old Mother Teresa?"

"Many times," Mickey said with a grin. "It's a burden I shoulder willingly."

Fifteen minutes before the game, Zoom and Mickey drifted down to left field to warm up. The stands were already filled and they were greeted by jeers and catcalls, which seemed to center on three themes:

1. The Orioles sucked.
2. Mickey was too fat.
3. Zoom was a traitor.

"You can feel the love, can't you?" Zoom noted drily as the howling increased. "Sounds like they really missed me."

"And apparently they want me to go on a diet," Mickey said. "Like that would ever happen." He looked down and patted his gut reassuringly.

They passed the small contingent of Orioles fans in the stands—Abby was standing on the top step of the bleachers, waving and snapping their picture on her cell phone—and went to work. Mickey marveled at how freely Zoom was throwing, and how hard, too. After twelve pitches, Zoom signaled that he was ready.

"You warm up faster than a microwave," Mickey said.

"Saving it for the game," Zoom said. "Arm feels good."

As they started back to the dugout, the taunting from the fans started up again. Zoom stopped and frowned. "I gotta admit, though, I'm pretty nervous. Not sure I've ever been so nervous."

"Me, too," Mickey said. "I think we all are. My dad said you'd have to be a zombie not to be nervous before a game like this."

Zoom took a deep breath and nodded.

"Do zombies throw up?" he asked. "'Cause I feel like I might puke."

"Don't know," Mickey said. "My parents won't let me watch *The Walking Dead*."

They looked at each other and laughed. At least for the moment, it helped them relax a little. But by the time both teams lined up along the first- and third-base foul lines for the national anthem, the Orioles were as grim-faced as Mickey had ever seen them.

He stole a glance across the diamond at the Yankees.

Money Mayhew was smiling broadly and rocking back and forth on his heels, looking like a man without a care in the world. Next to him stood his son, Moose. The big catcher stared balefully at the Orioles, chomping furiously on his gum and holding his cap over his heart as the final strains of the anthem sounded.

Just then Mickey felt a nudge in his ribs. Zoom was looking over at Moose, too.

"Look how he's holding his cap," Zoom whispered.

Mickey noticed it right away. Only one digit of Moose's hand was visible, outlined clearly against the dark cap.

Moose was giving them the finger.

"He's starting early," Zoom murmured. "Must've had an extra pregame Red Bull."

"Great," Mickey said. "Maybe he's so amped up he'll pass out."

"Not a chance," Zoom said.

A few minutes later, the Yankees took the field. Finally, it was game time. Hunter strode to the plate to lead off for the Orioles. Kevin Milo, the hard-throwing Yankees righty, finished his warm-up tosses and Moose threw down to second base. Then he jogged to the mound for a final chat with his pitcher.

As he shuffled back to his position, Moose stopped and glared at the Orioles dugout. Then he formed his thumb and forefinger into the shape of a gun and pretended to pull the trigger.

At first, the Orioles were so shocked that no one reacted.

Mickey felt a wave of despair come over him. Look at this, he thought. We're doing exactly what Zoom warned us not to do: letting the atmosphere get to us. Letting ourselves be intimidated by that big jerk before a single pitch is thrown.

In the next instant, Katelyn shot to her feet and cupped her hands around her mouth.

"MAR-VIN! MAR-VIN!" she began chanting.

The rest of the Orioles quickly picked it up. And now it was a singsong war cry, a full-throated statement of defiance. It was little David looking big, bad Goliath in the eye, pulling back the slingshot, and saying, *Okay, big guy, you want a fight? Let's go.*

"MAR-VIN! MAR-VIN! MAR-VIN!" The noise grew louder and louder.

Mickey looked around the dugout. All the Orioles were on their feet now, pointing at Moose and chanting. And standing next to Katelyn, shouting loudest of all, was Zoom.

Beautiful, Mickey thought.

Now we're ready to play some ball.

Moose whipped off his mask as the chant continued. His face was contorted with rage.

"Oh, it's definitely *on now!*" he screamed at the Orioles.

Mickey glanced at his dad, who stood in the third-base coach's box with a puzzled look on his face, as if to say, *Who the heck is Marvin?*

The Yankees fans started booing. A furious Money Mayhew popped out of their dugout and made a beeline for the umpire, gesturing at the Orioles.

The O's stopped chanting. But the noise from the crowd was so loud that it was hard to pick up what the Yankees coach was saying to the ump, who kept shrugging helplessly.

Then they heard the ump say, "How can I order them to stop chanting 'Marvin'? There's no rule against it. It's not exactly a swearword."

"It is in *this* dugout!" Katelyn cackled, earning a knock-it-off look from Mickey's dad.

Money was so beside himself that he yanked off his cap and slammed it to the ground. Then he kicked it and sent it sailing in the air a good fifteen feet. When he retrieved it, instead of returning it to his head, he slammed it to the ground again and proceeded to stomp on it like a man putting out a campfire.

The Orioles were laughing so hard they had tears in their eyes. But they were careful to hide their faces behind their gloves, not wanting to draw another death stare from Mickey's dad. It was by far the most astonishing temper tantrum any of them had ever seen from an adult.

When it was finally over, Money stalked back to the dugout, although not before pointing at Mickey's dad and shouting, "Can't you control your team, Coach? Is this how you teach your kids to play the game?"

"Oh, yeah," Sammy whispered. "Like the Yankees are the home office for good sportsmanship!"

"And like Moose didn't start it all by being a total dork!" Katelyn added.

Play finally got under way, and the Orioles got their first look at Kevin Milo. The Yankees big righty was throwing hard and his curve was the best the Orioles had faced all year—one of those curves that seemed so tantalizing at first and then broke sharply downward at the last minute.

He struck out Hunter on a breaking ball and got Katelyn on a soft line drive right at the third baseman. Sammy had a good at-bat, running the count to 3-and-2 and fouling off four straight pitches before he was badly fooled on another low curveball for strike three.

"Wear some earplugs," Sammy said when he trudged back to the dugout. "Moose is talking serious smack. He started in by saying I had an ugly girlfriend."

Mickey looked puzzled. "But . . . you don't even *have* a girlfriend," he said.

"I told him that," Sammy said. "So he called me a loser. For not having a girlfriend."

"Wow," Mickey said as he put on shin guards. "Tell him to make up his mind."

But in his head, Mickey knew that getting in a war of words with a master trash-talker like Moose was the worst thing a batter could do.

Number one, it would let Moose know he was getting to you, which would only make him yap even more. And number two, it distracted you from devoting your full attention to getting a hit. Which, after all, was the whole purpose of being up there.

No, Mickey thought, the only thing you could do with a motormouth like Moose was ignore him.

Which was like ignoring a loud, squawking parrot on your shoulder. But it had to be done.

Zoom was as sharp in the first inning for the Orioles as he'd been in pregame warm-ups. He had a determined look on his face and his fastball was ticking up around eighty miles an hour. Best of all, he didn't seem to be overthrowing.

He was clearly amped to be facing his old team. Now he was working fast and throwing strikes, just as every pitching coach on the planet preached. And when he struck out the lead-off batter, Mickey could tell by the expressions on the faces of the Yankees that they were impressed.

Impressed—and maybe even a little intimidated. Mickey guessed that they hadn't faced a pitcher as fast as

Zoom all season long. Sure, there were still a few players on the Yankees who remembered Zoom from the previous season, when he'd been a world-class jerk on a team populated by world-class jerks.

But even they were probably surprised by how smoothly and effortlessly he was throwing, how much his fastball moved, and how well he commanded his pitches.

The Yankees number two hitter tried to coax a walk, crouching low in the batter's box and jumping back theatrically with each pitch to make the ump think it was inside. But Zoom struck him out on four pitches, which set off a chorus of protest from Money Mayhew in the third-base coach's box.

"C'mon, blue!" he yelled. "Does one of my kids have to take one in the skull before you call a ball?"

Unbelievable, Mickey thought. It's only his team's second at-bat and already he's whining about the calls. Might be a new world's record.

But when Zoom struck out the next Yankee to end the inning, Money Mayhew trotted off the field with his head down and said nothing.

It was early, but both teams could sense how the game was shaping up. This one had all the makings of a good old-fashioned pitchers' duel: low scoring, pressure filled; one of those contests where the first team to blink and make a mistake loses.

The kind of game, Mickey thought, where your palms sweat the rest of the way. And his were already sweating.

Mainly because he was leading off this inning.

"Okay, let's go, let's go!" Mickey's dad said as Kevin Milo took his warm-up tosses. "Need some runs! What do we want to do at the plate against this guy?"

Katelyn and a few of the Orioles rolled their eyes.

"Coach," Katelyn said with a straight face, "should we be patient up there?"

"Should we look for our pitch?" Sammy chimed in.

"Should we remember a walk's as good as a hit?" Mickey added.

"Okay, okay," Mickey's dad said, grinning and throwing up his hands. "I get it. You've heard me say it a few times, huh?"

"More like a few thousand," Katelyn said. "In this month alone."

"Message received," Mickey's dad said, retreating to the third-base coach's box. "But it'd be nice to see one of you actually practice what I preach."

Moose grinned evilly when he saw Mickey coming to the plate.

"Whoa!" Moose cried. "Now here's a bi-i-i-g boy! Tell me something: Are you the catcher? Or did you, like, *eat* the catcher?"

Mickey felt his face get hot. But he vowed to ignore it.

White noise, he said to himself. Tune it out.

It wasn't easy. Moose kept up a low, steady stream of insults. Kevin Milo missed outside with two straight fastballs before Mickey swung and missed at a curve in the dirt.

He stepped out, angry at himself. Moose had him rattled, all right. Swinging at a garbage pitch like that—what was he thinking? The next pitch was another curveball, but

Mickey held up this time, sensing the pitch would miss low again.

Now it was 3-and-1. Hitter's count.

The noise level picked up. The Orioles were screaming and banging their bats against the bench. The Yankees fans were howling even louder. And Moose was barking like an angry pit bull in the background.

Kevin Milo peered in for the sign. He nodded, went into his windup, and now the pitch was on the way.

Fastball. And not a good one. It was coming in belt-high, without a lot of movement. Mickey's eyes lit up.

Level swing, hit it hard, put it in play—all of this ran through his mind in the fraction of a second he had to think. He kept his head still and turned on the ball. His hips, arms, and shoulders rotated perfectly and he caught it on the fat part of the bat.

The next time he looked up, the ball was soaring over the fence in left field.

Orioles 1, Yankees 0.

The Yankees looked stunned. Their fans were silent. Even Moose had quit yapping. Mickey wondered if he'd ever seen a sweeter sight than an arrogant team and its smug fan base humbled—at least for the moment—with one swing of the bat.

He took his time rounding the bases. What was the old saying his dad used about a slow home-run trot? You could time it with a sundial?

Exactly. This was one of those trots. But his dad didn't seem to mind. He wore a huge smile and slapped him a high five as he rounded third.

When Mickey finally crossed the plate, Moose whipped off his mask and spit at his feet.

"Three words, big boy," he snarled. "Luckiest. Shot. Ever."

Now Mickey couldn't contain himself. His body was pumping so hard with adrenaline he could feel it pulsing in his ears. He knew his dad would go crazy if he saw his kid trading smack with the other team.

But Mickey *had* to say something.

"Check the scoreboard—says you're a loser right now," he murmured as he turned for the dugout.

Moose snarled something back.

Just then, out of the corner of his eye, Mickey saw something flying in the big catcher's direction.

Moose went down in a heap.

The Yankees catcher jumped up right away. Blood gushed from his nose. He waved his fist and shouted angrily at Kevin Milo while the Orioles practically busted a gut trying not to laugh out loud.

"What happened?" Mickey asked when he reached the bench.

"Oh, you should have seen it!" Sammy whispered. "The pitcher wanted a new ball, right? So he tossed the old one to Moose. Only Moose wasn't paying attention. Too busy giving you a lot of crap. And the ball bopped him right on the nose."

"Talk about poetic justice," Hunter said.

The Orioles turned and stared at him.

"Nerd," Katelyn said, "do you even know what poetic justice *is*?"

"Of *course*," Hunter said. "It's a literary device. Good deeds rewarded, bad ones punished, etc. Everyone knows that."

The Orioles looked at one another in disbelief as Hunter smiled serenely.

"Nerd," Katelyn said, shaking her head, "you never cease to amaze me."

Now Money Mayhew popped out of the Yankees dugout with a worried look to check on his son. But Moose, holding his nose gingerly, waved him off.

"I'm *fine*, Dad!" he shouted. "Jeez! Way to overreact!"

The umpire pulled off his mask. "No, you're not fine, son," he said. "Can't play with a bloody nose. League rule. Gotta clean yourself up."

This time Money returned with a first-aid kit. He wiped the blood from his son's face with a cloth and handed him two strips of cotton gauze. Moose rolled them into tiny cylinders and shoved one in each nostril.

"Ewww, gross!" Katelyn said. "He looks like a walrus with those things sticking out of his nose!"

But the umpire checked Moose again and seemed satisfied the bleeding was under control. "Let's play ball—again!" he cried. Moose glared at his pitcher once more before pulling down his mask and dropping into his crouch.

Kevin Milo was clearly shaken now, presumably from both Mickey's homer and his own role in the near maiming of his all-star catcher. He walked around the mound, trying to compose himself as Corey dug in and the Orioles dugout got even louder.

Yet even though the Orioles hit the ball hard off the Yankees pitcher, each shot went right at someone. Corey hit a rocket to the third baseman, who was perfectly positioned near the line, and Spencer and Ethan both flied out to deep left field to end the threat.

"One run's not enough to win this," Gabe said worriedly

before the O's took the field. "Not the way these monsters hit. And by the way? Your buddy Moose leads off."

When Moose swaggered to the plate, Mickey looked at him and did a double take. The cotton gauze was gone from Moose's nostrils. But his nose was red and swollen to twice its size, making his eyes squint and his face look distorted.

The kid looks like a completely different person! Mickey thought. No, check that. With that huge nose, he doesn't even look like a *person*.

He looks like . . . Mr. Potato Head!

"What're you staring at?" Moose growled as he dug in.

Just checking out your new look, handsome, Mickey wanted to say. But Zoom was already peering in for the sign, so he refocused on the game and said nothing.

Zoom pitched Moose carefully—a little *too* carefully, Mickey thought. He blew a fastball past the big catcher, but then missed with two straight curves and a fastball outside.

Three-and-1. Zoom had gotten himself in a dangerous count. Moose stepped out and made a big show of loosening and tightening his batting gloves before stepping back in.

As soon as the next pitch left Zoom's hand, Mickey winced.

It was going to be low. He dropped to his knees, ready to smother it in the dirt. Oh, well, he thought. A walk to this guy isn't the worst thing in the world.

Except in the next instant, Moose reached down with what looked like a golf swing and sent the ball rocketing over the center-field fence.

The big scoreboard flashed: Orioles 1, Yankees 1.

Zoom looked stricken. As the Yankees fans erupted,

Moose rounded the bases with his fist thrust in the air. Nearing home, he jumped and came crashing down on the plate with both feet while pointing gleefully at Mickey as if to say, *Your turn to check the score, dude.*

Okay, fine, Mickey thought.

But you still look like Mr. Potato Head.

As the Yankees poured out of the dugout to high-five Moose, Zoom wore a disgusted expression. Mickey jogged out to the mound.

"How did he hit that?" Zoom asked. "Crappiest pitch I've ever thrown, and the kid just flicks his bat and—"

Mickey tried to keep his voice calm.

"Sometimes you gotta give the other team credit," he said. "They're trying to win, too. Now forget it. Get the next guy."

Zoom managed a wan smile. "Okay, Coach," he said. "You're right. We move on."

Just as Kevin Milo had, Zoom seemed to recover quickly. He struck out the next two batters. The third kid up put a good swing on a fastball, but Corey made a terrific diving catch of a sinking line drive to center to end the inning.

"Awesome glove, C!" Mickey's dad shouted as the O's ran off the field. "Need some offense now!"

But from there, the game turned into a pitching clinic. Both Zoom and Kevin Milo were throwing hard, mixing their pitches and keeping the hitters off balance.

Moose was still chirping at the Orioles batters and Money Mayhew was still barking at the umps and keeping up a loud running commentary that tended to disparage the O's.

"Watch out for this guy now," he yelled to his team the next time Hunter was up. "He doesn't look like much, kind of scrawny and all. But you never know."

The game was still tied at one in the sixth inning when the Orioles came to bat. Mickey could feel the tension in the dugout. It had been building with each scoreless inning. Katelyn plopped down next to him with a worried look.

"You realize that if—" she said before Mickey cut her off with a wave of his hand.

Yes, he thought, everyone on the team knows the situation.

If the game went extra innings, Zoom would have to come out. A kid could only pitch six innings in a game, even in the playoffs. Which meant that Danny would come on in relief. And with his mediocre fastball, it would be like batting practice for the Yankees.

Whereas the Yankees' number two pitcher threw almost as hard as Kevin Milo. So did their number three pitcher, for that matter.

"Don't think about it," Mickey said. "We get a run here, and Zoom closes out the win—that's how I'm looking at it."

Katelyn seemed to relax.

"Mr. Positive!" she said. "That's good! I like the way you think, nerd!"

Mickey smiled and the two of them bumped fists. He wasn't sure he felt as positive as he sounded—not that Katelyn needed to know that.

But Kevin Milo was still dominating and the Orioles went down in order in the sixth. Now the pressure was squarely on Zoom—again.

"One more inning," Mickey said, clapping him on the back as the two took the field.

Zoom took a deep breath and nodded. "I got this," he said.

After all the pitches he'd thrown on a hot, humid July night, Zoom was still masterful.

He struck out the first Yankees batter on three straight fastballs. The second batter managed to foul off a couple of pitches before hitting a weak bouncer to Ethan at first.

Two outs. Coming to the plate now for the Yankees was Kevin Milo.

According to Zoom's scouting report, Milo was a pretty good hitter. But Mickey was happy to see him anyway. Nice way to finish the first six innings, Mickey thought. Two great pitchers going at it like gladiators until the end.

Was this poetic justice, too? Mickey wasn't sure. But it felt right.

Zoom went right at Kevin from the start. He blew a chest-high fastball past him. Kevin was fooled badly on Zoom's second pitch, another fastball, and lifted a foul ball into the stands.

Oh-and-2. Things were looking good.

Kevin hit a sharp grounder to third. Hunter was positioned perfectly. He crouched and tapped his glove calmly and got ready to gather it in.

Mickey felt himself relax. We did it, he thought. Made it to extra innings.

Except . . . suddenly the ball took a bizarre hop and shot over Hunter's shoulder.

It caught the back seam of the infield grass and squirted

into foul territory in left field. Then it rolled around the fence for what seemed like an eternity as Spencer, who'd been playing deep with two outs, charged it.

Finally it died in the thick grass against two wooden slats.

By the time Spencer retrieved it, Kevin was flying past third base and heading for home. Spencer made a strong throw, a one-hopper that Mickey gloved just in front of the plate. Whirling around, he lunged and tagged Kevin on the thigh as he slid across the plate.

"SAFE!" the umpire cried.

Game over.

Final score: Yankees 2, Orioles 1.

The season was officially over.

As the Yankees poured out of their dugout to celebrate, with their fans storming the field, the Orioles looked on in shock. Then they filed quietly into their dugout and slumped on the bench with their heads hanging. Katelyn sat pale and seething in one corner.

For a long time, no one spoke.

Finally Zoom said softly, "Okay, this may sound weird. But that's the most fun I ever had playing baseball."

Mickey studied his pitcher for a moment. Was Zoom serious? Mickey could see that he was. Slowly the big catcher nodded in agreement. "Lots of crazy stuff happened, that's for sure."

"Like Moose getting bopped in the nose!" Sammy blurted.

"And his dad flipping out on the ump and doing the Mexican hat dance!" Hunter chimed in.

"And the stupid ball taking a crazy bounce over you!" Justin said. "Like someone had programmed it in a video game!"

The rest of the team started to perk up.

"A lot of *good* stuff happened, too," Gabe said. "You pitched a great game, Z. Nine out of ten times, we'd get a win if you pitched like that."

"How about Corey's catch?" Ethan said. "That was *money*! Lays out in midair and snags that bad boy!"

"What about Mickey's homer, nerds?" Katelyn said. They were happy to see the color return to her face.

"No, Moose's was *way* better," Mickey said. "That kid is strong! He may be a jerk, but he can send the ball a long way. Even with a Mr. Potato Head nose!"

By now the Orioles were laughing and trading fist bumps and talking excitedly about everything that had happened in the past two hours. By the time Mickey's dad clambered down the steps, most of the postgame shock and gloom had lifted.

He held up his hands for quiet.

"Two things," he said. "First, I'm so proud of you guys. I hope you remember this game for the rest of your lives. And second, I just finished talking with Coach Mayhew."

The Orioles booed loudly.

"No, hear me out," Mickey's dad continued. "He said you guys played a great game and they were lucky to win. And get this: he said the Orioles were the best team the Yankees faced all season!"

The dugout erupted in cheers, drawing curious stares

from the Yankees players and fans who were still mingling on the field.

One of the players was Moose. Face still puffy, he glared and pointed to the scoreboard.

"What*ever*, Marvin," Katelyn murmured. "And do something about that nose. You're scaring people."

The Orioles laughed and hooted and fist-bumped one another again, the noise sounding like the biggest party any of them had ever attended.

Mickey took in the raucous scene and smiled.

Zoom was right, he thought.

This was *the best game ever. No matter what the scoreboard said.*

The phone rang at ten o'clock the next morning, just as Mickey was blasting through the high desert at a hundred miles per hour in a sick-looking dune buggy with a flaming-orange paint job. He stared at the screen and gripped the controller even tighter.

"No!" he yelled at the phone. "Stop ringing!"

Now he was shooting through a red sandstone ravine, the mutant alien pack chasing him furiously, tires screeching, exhaust fumes swirling, ATVs and dirt bikes spinning out behind him, except . . . the phone was still ringing.

"I can't hear you!" he yelled as he swerved around a massive boulder. But his parents were out shopping and they'd told him to take a message if anyone called.

"This better be important," he muttered.

He threw down the controller and looked at the phone. The caller ID said: ELLIOTT, ABIGAIL.

He felt his heart quicken. Okay, he thought. *Definitely* important.

As usual, there wasn't a lot of preliminary chitchat from Abby, which was fine with Mickey.

"I'm at the snowball stand, star," Abby said. "Stop by if you have a moment."

"I have a moment," Mickey said. "In fact, I have many moments. Baseball season's over, remember? Right now I'm exercising my intellectual capabilities, playing *Roadkill Three: Into the Chaos*."

Abby groaned. He could picture her behind the counter, frowning with disapproval at his choice of pastimes as she nervously scanned for bees.

"Is that the game with the stupid alien bikers?" she asked. "Who, like, have three eyes and seven arms and nine legs? That game will rot your brain."

"Not much left to rot," Mickey said. "The aliens were about to run me down anyway. And have me for dinner. See you in a few."

It was a great morning for a bike ride. The sun shone brightly and the humidity of the previous day was mostly gone. Large puffy clouds seemed to race across the clear blue sky. When he got to the field and pulled up to the stand, he broke into a big smile.

There, to one side of the stone walkway, was a large handmade sign that read in big, block letters: GREAT SEASON, DULANEY ORIOLES! WE'RE PROUD OF YOU!

Flanking it was another sign: 1 FREE SNOWBALL FOR EACH TEAM MEMBER! SATURDAY ONLY!

A handful of the Orioles were already there. Zoom was snapping photos of the two signs with his cell phone. "I *gotta* get one of those," Mickey muttered for the umpteenth time. Once again he envisioned himself as a seventeen-year-old loser in high school who *still* had to use a landline to call his friends, thanks to his mom and dad.

Katelyn, Sammy, and Gabe were grumbling about school starting in three weeks while Abby was cheerfully bustling about making snowballs for everyone.

"I told my boss I'd pay for these myself," she was explaining now. "But she said no, you guys deserve some freebies after that great game last night."

"Freebies for losers!" Sammy crowed. "Imagine if we ever beat the Yankees! Your boss would probably take us to a five-star restaurant!"

"Where *you'd* probably order McNuggets," Katelyn said to laughter.

"I sure don't feel like a loser," Zoom said, and the others nodded in agreement. "I kept replaying that game over and over in my head on the ride home. We have nothing to be ashamed of. In fact, we were awesome!"

Now Abby seemed to grow pensive.

"Can I ask you guys a question?" she said. "Do you believe in destiny?"

The Orioles looked at one another and shrugged.

"Because to work so hard and come so close to winning last night," she continued, "and then to have that crazy grounder shoot over Hunter . . . it felt almost like the final outcome was decided ahead of time."

No one said anything at first.

Then, with a serious look on his face, Mickey said, "You want to know what I think about destiny?"

The rest of them listened intently.

"Okay, I think it's my destiny to be at Augie's on Monday for Wing Night," he said. "And furthermore, I think it's my destiny to try the honey-barbecue sauce this time. Might even go wild and have the mango-habanero, too."

As the Orioles cracked up again, Katelyn said, "And Zoom, now that you're not the world's biggest, self-centered dork anymore, you're officially invited."

"Thanks . . . I think," Zoom said. "That's about the weirdest invitation I've ever gotten."

"You should come, too, Abby," Mickey said. "As 'Snowball Maker to the Stars,' you're practically a member of the team now."

"Yeah," Katelyn said. She jerked a thumb at Mickey. "Then you can watch this one gross everyone out with his eating habits."

Abby smiled at Mickey. "I'd love to go," she said, and Mickey could feel his face getting warm.

"Which brings up another matter," Abby continued. "Guess what? My dad said I could play baseball next year if I want to."

"Get *out!*" Mickey said. "Hey, that's great!"

"Yeah, I've been working on him for a while," Abby said. "He was always afraid to let me play. He thought baseball was too dangerous. Way more dangerous than softball, with the ball being so much smaller and harder."

"What made him change his mind?" Mickey asked.

"I think I just wore him down," Abby said. "Plus, he saw how exciting your game was last night. And how much I want to be part of something like that."

"So you're definitely playing baseball?" Zoom asked.

"Well," she said, "I'm seriously thinking about it."

"Come play for us," Katelyn said. "We could totally use

another girl on this team. It would automatically lower the nerd factor, for one thing."

"Are you saying there aren't any girl nerds?" Sammy said. "Because that's ridiculous. I see them all the time."

"For your information," Katelyn said, "the ratio of boy nerds to girl nerds is like ten to one. Maybe twenty to one. You could look it up."

"Where do you look up something like that?" Gabe wondered. "Nerdipedia?"

As a fresh wave of laughter engulfed them, Abby pulled Mickey aside.

"Okay, star, you didn't get your snowball yet," she said. "What exotic flavor are you going with today? No, never mind. Let me take a wild guess."

She grabbed a plastic cup, filled it with shaved ice, and moved toward the grape bottle.

"Whoa!" Mickey said. "Easy with the high-pressure sales tactics! Don't I get a minute to decide?"

Abby watched him warily as he made a big show of studying the flavor menu.

"After long and careful deliberation," he said finally, "I'm going to go with—ta-da!—Atomic Apple and Caramel."

Abby put her hands on her hips. "We don't *have* Atomic Apple and Caramel," she said evenly.

Mickey frowned.

"Oh, that's disappointing," he said. "That's *very* disappointing. Okay, then make it grape."

As Mickey cackled gleefully, Abby rolled her eyes.

"If we're teammates next year and I have to put up with this," she said, "it'll be a long, *long* season."

If you enjoyed this book, look for

THE CLOSER

a novel by
CAL RIPKEN, JR.
with Kevin Cowherd

As soon as the pitch left his hand, Danny Connolly thought, Uh-oh.

The ball had come off his sweat-slicked fingers all wrong. Now it was floating gently to the plate, a weak waist-high fastball destined to be launched into orbit—possibly all the way to the International Space Station—by the glowering Red Sox batter.

Maybe the kid won't swing, Danny thought. Maybe he'll be so shocked at how lame the pitch is that he'll just burst out laughing.

But that was wishful thinking.

No, the boy's eyes were lighting up already, like it was a bacon-and-cheese-stuffed pizza sailing toward him. His hips were starting to turn. His shoulders were uncoiling. His bat was moving forward.

Danny winced. This was not going to be good.

What followed was a loud *PING!* that sounded like a coin dropped on a dinner plate. By the time he whipped his head around, the ball was arching over the left-field fence for a three-run homer, and the kid was doing a slow trot around the bases—slow enough to wave to his mother, his sisters and brothers, his grandparents, and every other person in the stands.

Bet he even waves to his dog, Danny thought, kicking at the dirt in disgust.

He looked at the scoreboard and sighed. Red Sox 4, Orioles 1. So much for following Coach's instructions.

"Just hold 'em this inning and we'll find a way to win," Coach had said, handing Danny the ball, clapping him on the back, and flashing a smile that was meant to be reassuring.

Danny stole a quick glance at the Orioles dugout. No, Coach wasn't smiling anymore. Instead, he looked as if someone had just rear-ended his car.

Even before the umpire fished another ball from his pocket, Sammy Noah, the Orioles shortstop, called time and jogged to the mound. He was followed by Ethan Novitsky, the rangy first baseman.

Neither of them looked happy.

"What . . . was *that*?" Sammy said.

Danny hung his head.

"I know, I know. . . ." he said. "My bad. Ugly pitch."

"*Seriously* ugly," Ethan said. "My little brother throws harder than that."

Danny managed a weak smile.

"Can you get your little brother on your phone?" Danny asked. "We may need him, the way this is going."

The two boys just stared at him.

"What?" Danny said. "Not the time for jokes?"

"Uh, probably not," Sammy said. "Instead of working on your lines, work on getting this next guy out, okay?"

He looked at Ethan and the two rolled their eyes before heading back to their positions.

As he bent down and grabbed the resin bag, it occurred to Danny that sometimes jokes were the only thing that kept his spirits up in games like this.

The truth was, he was having a crappy season so far as the Orioles backup pitcher. Oh, he knew what *backup* meant, of course. *Backup* meant not good enough to start. *Backup* meant we'll get you in there when we can, kid. Now zip it and grab some bench.

And with hard-throwing Zach "Zoom" Winslow on the team, a tall right-hander who could touch 80 mph on the radar gun, Danny knew the O's had a marquee starter who was one of the top pitchers in the league. Not to mention way better than Danny.

Which he could live with—at least for now.

The problem was, when he *did* get into games, Danny hadn't exactly been a shutdown reliever either.

That's what Danny wanted to be: the closer. When he went with his family to Camden Yards to watch the big-league Orioles play, he loved seeing the bullpen doors swing open in the ninth inning of a tight game and Zach Britton, their closer, come strutting out to the mound.

With the crowd on its feet and cheering madly, the closer would chomp furiously on his gum, glare at the batters, and blow them away one-two-three to preserve the win.

The closer came in to put out the fire—everyone knew that. But in his last five or six outings, Danny had been hit hard. And when he wasn't hit hard, he'd given up way too many walks.

He sure hadn't been putting out any fires. In fact, his teammates were starting to call him "Gas Can" Connolly for his habit of taking the mound and making the fire worse.

Great, Danny thought. A horrible new nickname to haunt me for the rest of the season.

Things were going so badly that, warming up in his backyard earlier in the afternoon, he'd even sailed a pitch over the bounce-back net and shattered a window in his next-door neighbor's house.

Cranky old Mr. Spinelli hadn't been home at the time, which was a lucky break. And Danny had slipped a note under the man's front door, taking responsibility for the accident. But he knew the gloomy geezer would go thermo-nuclear once he spotted all that broken glass.

Oh, well, he thought. I'll worry about that later.

He took a deep breath and tried to refocus on the Red Sox. Two outs. One more and at least they'd be out of the inning.

As the next batter dug in, Danny peered in for the sign from Mickey Labriogla, the O's catcher. Mickey put down three fingers: changeup.

Danny couldn't believe his eyes. A *changeup*? What was the plan here—to just *give* the game away?

To bore the other team to death?

Here he'd just thrown possibly the slowest pitch ever recorded in the history of youth baseball, and the batter had crushed it. And now his catcher was calling for *another* off-speed pitch? Another meatball that might end up in yet another galaxy far, far away?

Why don't we just throw underhand from now on?

Then he caught himself. Maybe Mickey knew something about the batter that Danny didn't. Maybe Mickey knew the kid was so geeked to swing for the fences that he might screw himself into the ground with some slow junk.

In any event, Danny wasn't about to shake off his catcher, who also happened to be the best catcher in the league and Coach's son. He nodded, took a deep breath, and went into his windup.

One changeup coming up.

PING!

This time the batter lashed a towering drive into the gap in right center. Danny's heart sank as he watched center fielder Corey Maduro and right fielder Katelyn Morris turn and race after it.

But at the last moment, it was Katelyn who ran it down, making a lunging over-the-shoulder catch before tumbling to the ground and raising her glove high to show she had the ball.

As the Orioles fans in the stands cheered wildly, Danny breathed a sigh of relief and headed for the dugout.

"Saved your butt—*again*," Katelyn hissed as the Orioles hustled off the field. "You totally owe me, nerd."

Good ol' Katelyn, Danny thought, shaking his head.

Encouraging as ever. Always ready to pick you up when you're feeling down.

Danny took a seat on the bench, and Mickey plopped down beside him. The big catcher's bushy red hair was plastered to his forehead with sweat. He grabbed a towel and began wiping his face.

"I wonder if I might make a suggestion," he began.

"If it's 'Why don't you give up pitching and take up the tuba,' I'm way ahead of you," Danny said dejectedly. "And I'm not even sure I could *lift* a tuba, let alone play it."

Mickey grinned and shook his head.

"No, my suggestion is this: next time I call for a changeup in that situation, you call time, okay? Then walk to the plate and smack me upside the head."

Danny looked up and saw that Mickey's eyes were twinkling. This was the great thing about the O's catcher: win or lose, he was always in a great mood. Which was why he was one of Danny's best friends.

No one loved the game more than Mickey did. And this, Danny knew, was Mickey's way of trying to make him feel better. The big guy was taking some of the blame for the near-disastrous consequences of that last pitch.

Danny couldn't help but grin, too.

"Deal," he said, and the two bumped fists.

"Good," Mickey said. "One more thing: you throw nothing but fastballs next inning, okay? No matter how many fat little fingers I put down. Just throw hard and don't worry about it."

But the sixth inning was almost as rocky for Danny as the previous one. He struggled with his control from the outset. He walked the first two batters before giving up a ground-rule double, the ball skipping over the fence and nearly hitting an old man in a straw hat and sunglasses who was watching from the shade of a tree.

A comebacker to the mound and a nice catch by first baseman Ethan Novitsky in foul territory kept the Red Sox runner at second base before Danny struck out the leadoff batter to end the inning. But the damage was done. And when the Orioles failed to rally in their half of the inning, Danny found himself feeling even worse.

Final score: Red Sox 6, Orioles 1.

It was their second loss in a row, and third in the last five games. As he listened to Coach's postgame remarks—it was the usual stuff about keeping their heads up and working hard and blah, blah, blah—Danny realized with a jolt that his lousy pitching had played a major role in all three of the team's losses.

The thought nearly made him sick to his stomach.

Mickey, Katelyn, and some of the others were going for ice cream, but Danny couldn't bring himself to join them and fake being in a good mood. Instead, he gathered up his gear, trudged out to the parking lot, and plunked himself down on the curb to wait for his mom.

At dusk, her SUV finally pulled in. When she rolled up next to him and powered down the window, he could see she was beaming.

Here it comes, he thought.

"Joey was awesome this afternoon!" his mom said.

Of course he was, Danny thought. Joey's *always* awesome.

"They beat the other team—the Titans, I think it was—five–nothing," she went on. "Your brother threw a three-hitter."

Hmm, Danny thought. Only a three-hitter? Must have the flu or something.

"The other team didn't have a prayer," his mom said. "Oh, Joey didn't have his best game. But he still struck out nine."

Danny cocked an eyebrow. Under double-digits in K's, too? Get that kid to the emergency room!

He threw his gear in the backseat and climbed in. Pulling on his seat belt, he counted down silently: three, two, one. As if on cue, his mom launched into a play-by-play of Joey's Metro League game as they pulled out onto the highway and headed home.

"Joey seemed a little nervous in the first inning, maybe because of all the scouts . . ." she began.

This had become her routine since Joey's terrific junior season in high school had ended two months earlier, after he'd posted a glittering 8–0 record and college recruiters and pro scouts began appearing at his games.

Now that he was playing summer ball and lighting up the league for the Mid-Atlantic Marauders, his games often fell on the same night as Danny's. But both his mom and dad had been spending the bulk of their time at Joey's games, swept up in the excitement of their older son's exploits. And when Joey's games were over, it was usually his mom who was dispatched to pick up Danny.

On these nights, with her younger son trapped in the front seat beside her, she'd invariably launch into what Danny called "The All About Joey Hour."

"Your dad said there were at least four scouts there," she continued. "Plus there were two other guys with clip-boards along the right-field fence. . . ."

Danny shook his head softly. *Clipboards?* They didn't even have iPads? What kind of loser organizations did they work for?

"Anyway, Joey's fastball was all over the place at first," his mom droned on. "But then he started to settle down. And by the second inning he was really locked in. . . ."

Danny stared straight ahead at the traffic on I-83. As usual, he quickly tuned his mom out. He'd been listening to this stuff for weeks and considered it a uniquely painful form of torture, given how badly he himself was pitching.

It was not until they were on York Road, only a few miles from home, that his mom glanced over and realized her younger son had yet to say a word.

"Oh, I'm so sorry, sweetie," she said, shaking her head. "Didn't even ask about your game. How awful of me! Tell me how the Orioles did."

Danny looked out the window. The truth was, he loved seeing how happy his mom was after Joey threw a good game, how proud she seemed. He never wanted to spoil these moments. After all, he was as proud and happy for his brother as anyone else.

"We lost to the Red Sox," he said finally. "But it's okay. Coach said we played well. He didn't kill anybody in his little talk after the game."

His mother nodded and smiled. "And how did my favorite Oriole do? Get to pitch?"

Danny stared out at the darkness again. What was the point of getting into all that now? Why tell her that her younger son—good ol' Gas Can himself—had come on in relief of Zoom and turned a smoldering trash-can fire into a towering inferno?

"I pitched a couple of innings," he said with a shrug. "Did okay, I guess."

Yes, it was a white lie. But he didn't want to watch his mom's face cloud over with concern, as it always did when she heard he hadn't pitched well. The way she looked at him—you'd think he'd just been diagnosed with a terminal illness.

She reached over and patted him on the arm.

"I'm sure you did just fine," she said. Then, after a pause: "Now, in the fourth inning, Joey had to face the middle of their batting order...."

Danny sighed. Up ahead, he could see the streetlamps winking on as they turned into his neighborhood.

But "The All About Joey Hour" was still going strong. And as usual, there were no commercial interruptions.